P9-APC-994

"Did you 'see' the kind of woman I am, or not?"

Rowan's voice was strangled as she asked the question. She could not have fought free if he had not suddenly released her.

"Up to a point," Dario drawled. "To where you showed that you do come in two layers—an outraged frigidity on top and a latent sensuality that you deny underneath. What, if anything new, did you learn about me?"

"Nothing more than that you're an opportunist as well as a sadist," she flung at him.

"Frankly, would you say that in the matter of moral tarnish, there's much to choose between us," he retorted.

Rowan turned away without answering. Though she had told Dario she despised him, was it possible that some unbidden urge within her had wanted to respond to the hard mastery of his hands and lips?

Jane Arbor is one of Harlequin's veteran authors. Her first romance, *City Nurse*, was published in 1958. Eight years and many romances later, came *A Girl Named Smith*, which holds the distinction of being Harlequin's one thousandth title. These two books and the book you are now holding were all written in the same "white-walled, black-beamed, Anne Hathaway thatched cottage" north of the Thames River that has been Jane's home for more than thirty years. It's an enchanting spot where, above everything else, she enjoys "writing books that people want to read."

Books by Jane Arbor

HARLEQUIN ROMANCE

Don't miss any of our special offers. Write to us at the following address for information on our newest releases.

Harlequin Reader Service
901 Fuhrmann Blvd., P.O. Box 1397, Buffalo, NY 14240
Canadian address: P.O. Box 603,
Fort Erie, Ont. L2A 5X3

House of Discord

Jane Arbor

Harlequin Books

TORONTO • NEW YORK • LONDON
AMSTERDAM • PARIS • SYDNEY • HAMBURG
STOCKHOLM • ATHENS • TOKYO • MILAN

Original hardcover edition published in 1983
by Mills & Boon Limited

ISBN 0-373-17003-3

Harlequin Romance first edition December 1987

Copyright © 1983 by Jane Arbor.
Philippine copyright 1983. Australian copyright 1983.
All rights reserved. Except for use in any review, the reproduction or utilization
of this work in whole or in part in any form by any electronic, mechanical
or other means, now known or hereafter invented, including xerography,
photocopying and recording, or in any information storage or retrieval system,
is forbidden without the permission of the publisher, Harlequin Enterprises
Limited, 225 Duncan Mill Road, Don Mills, Ontario, Canada M3B 3K9. All the
characters in this book have no existence outside the imagination of the
author and have no relation whatsoever to anyone bearing the same name
or names. They are not even distantly inspired by any individual known
or unknown to the author, and all incidents are pure invention.

The Harlequin trademarks, consisting of the words HARLEQUIN ROMANCE
and the portrayal of a Harlequin, are trademarks of Harlequin Enterprises
Limited; the portrayal of a Harlequin is registered in the United States Patent
and Trademark Office and in the Canada Trade Marks Office.

Printed in U.S.A.

CHAPTER ONE

'*Then who is this child?*'

Rowan looked down to stare at the coloured snapshot being thrust into her hand. It was of a toddler with spade and pail on a beach, a small boy whom she had never seen before. She shook her head in blank bewilderment. 'I don't know,' she faltered.

With something near a snarl of disbelief the snapshot was snatched back. 'You claim this is not your son?'

'I do.'

'You deny that you have a child by Leone? *This* one, in fact ... name of Scipio, now aged three?' A fingernail rapped the glossy print like a pistol shot, and a hand gripped Rowan's shoulder, shaking it. The dark accented voice continued relentlessly, 'You are lying, of course. Therefore, now let us hear it all again, may we?— but for the truth this time, please.'

The cold April day had begun like any other. As often happened now Rowan had wakened early to worry—that, as from Easter just past, she had no job and nothing yet in view. Six months ago after Leone's death had widowed her, the days had always been shadowed by regrets and loneliness. But now these too-early waking thoughts had to be for her own survival in a working world, and she needed to rally her spirits by counting her blessings, such as they were.

She was a qualified secretary, wasn't she?— with particular experience in the routine of schools. Both the jobs she had had since college and throughout her marriage to Leone had been day-school posts, the latest having folded at the end of the Lent term only because of the amalgamation of her school with a larger one where there was staff, including a headmaster's secretary, to take over both.

She had testimonials and could call upon others. She had savings and there was the money which had been in Leone's bank. She was virtually alone in the world with no dependants. If things had been ... different between her and Leone (her mind always baulked at expressing this thought), she might by now have had a child or children to care for, and she had learned— almost—to stifle regrets and longings by trying to see her childlessness as one more blessing to count.

Sometimes, particularly when Leone refused to discuss it with her, she had wondered whether she would have married him had he admitted in time his inability to father children. From the saner plane of marriage it was difficult to get back into the heart and head of the twenty-year-old

Rowan Burke who had fallen so irrevocably to the passionate rush of courtship from the debonair sophisticated Italian, Leone Cortese, met informally in a concert queue and recognised very quickly as the first real love of her life.

He hadn't claimed—she wouldn't have believed him if he had—that she was *his* first love. He was over thirty, darkly handsome and experienced, the elder son of two in the direct line of a proud Roman family counting its ancestry through many generations and troubled centuries. To be a Cortese of Rome, Rowan gathered, was to walk very tall indeed, and she hadn't doubted Leone could command and conduct a love affair anywhere he pleased. But he had chosen to marry *her*, a London working girl, simply because, he had claimed, she had a complexion like fresh cream, a boyish cap of gold-bronze hair, the figure of a ballet dancer, and laughed when he did, and at the same things.

Perhaps it shouldn't have been reason enough for her to accept him. But for her, then, it was. It was only later, when it would have been too late if she hadn't still loved him, that some raw facts about Leone's character and career had emerged, smirching the picture of him as the accepted heir to the Cortese private estate and the ownership and management of great parcels of properties in and around the city. He had quarrelled with his family, rebelling against a 'mere landlord career'; had flung away, first to Paris, and then to

London, his chief interest being in the motoring world, and had been virtually cut off by his father, Leopoldo Cortese, in consequence.

Leopoldo had a second son as dedicated and family-orientated as himself. So let brother Dario take over the job of building, and rehousing and placating tenants, and though there was money in it, Leone had allowed, Dario was welcome to it, since he, Leone, had got himself and taken to wife the sweetest little *bambina* in London, and was content with his bargain, he boasted.

Something of sour grapes there? But Rowan hadn't questioned it aloud. *She* was content too, even though, at least during their first year of marriage, the motoring world of sales and shows and demonstrations hadn't served Leone any too well financially. After that, money had been easier. She had kept on her job and Leone, though he didn't seem much busier, had more cash of his own to spend.

It was then, when it seemed they had security which would continue, that Rowan allowed herself some nesting thoughts and began to tease Leone that wasn't it time they soldered their Italo-British alliance with a Cortese baby? Or two in due course? Or twins in one fell swoop—why not?

She was not to forget the day when he told her there was no hope of that . . . She hadn't believed him; had protested that he couldn't *know*. Doctors weren't always right! But she hadn't any argument against the facts Leone had quoted.

For as far back as the Corteses traced their ancestry the eldest son in the direct line had produced no heirs, and Leone, warned as soon as he was adult, had no reason to hope the curse would be broken through him.

'Your father?' Rowan had questioned faintly.

'*His* father's second son. His elder brother, Uncle Alban, went into the priesthood. He is dead now,' said Leone.

'So that your brother Dario——?'

'—isn't married. Before I left Rome he was carrying a torch for our cousin, Andrea Vancusa, but she married someone else.' Downcast and contrite, Leone reached to take Rowan into his arms. 'I ought to have told you, *carissima*. But I couldn't risk losing you. And does it matter so very much, after all? I broke free of the Cortese cobwebs when I split, and isn't it enough that we have each other? Dear, *dear* little London sparrow—'pecking little kisses at her ear, her nose-tip, her lips—'tell your cruel, cowardly Leone that it is?'

Loving him, she had told him, and only once later had ventured to suggest that they might adopt. But Leone wouldn't hear of it, wouldn't discuss it.

They never had, between then and the terrible day last November when Leone had died. Rowan supposed she should be thankful now, but at heart she wasn't. Leone had left her little but his name, and that she could never pass on . . .

On this day-like-any-other she had done some shopping in the morning, lunched on soup and a salad, with the newspaper propped against the water jug, and was writing yet another job application when the apartment doorbell rang.

Now who? The afternoon had darkened early, and the figure of the man at the door she opened was only in silhouette to the storm clouds behind him.

She looked a question at him. He said, 'Signora Leone Cortese? Dario Cortese, Leone's brother. May I come in?'

After all this time! Her letter addressed to Conte Leopoldo Cortese telling of Leone's death had gone unanswered, as had Leone's letter informing his father of their marriage four years ago. She had concluded that the Corteses had nothing to say to her of sympathy or compassion and she had practically written them out of her thoughts. Yet here was this stranger, seeking her out, looking for her acceptance of him. On what errand? she wondered, as she stood back with the frosty welcome, 'I see. Please do,' and made a gesture towards taking his coat, which he ignored.

She led the way, turned to face him in her living-room—and caught her breath with shock.

It was Leone who stood there in the virile flesh which death had snatched from him. There was the same spare elegance and height, the same fluid movement of body, the same darkness of hair and feature, the same narrow face formed by thin bones and taut muscles, the same patrician head-high air. But with a difference ... This face, she felt sure, couldn't light up and break into Leone's urchin smile. The pull of the lines etched from nostrils to mouth-corners was too grim and hard. When Dario Cortese laughed it would be cruelly, or derisively, without mirth, she thought. If his appearance told the truth, there was little of yielding softness in him.

How right she was, she was soon to find out. He waited for her to sit, then took the chair she indicated. 'You are surprised to see me, *signora*?' he asked.

'Yes. My letter to Leone's father wasn't answered.'

'No, but there was a reason. He had a massive heart attack at the time and couldn't be consulted.'

'But since?'

'He has recovered, but wasn't willing to make the decision to send me to you until now. You speak Italian, *signora*?'

'Of course. Leone taught it to me and we used it regularly.' Rowan didn't see why she should confide to the cold mask opposite how their courtship had been hilariously conducted in broken phrases from each language.

The mask was asking, 'But you would prefer we talk in English?'

'I think so. I am—six months out of practice in Italian.'

A nod and a long assessing stare. Then Dario said, 'I find you more self-possessed, *signora*, than I'd have expected in a young widow of only six months. Is that a control that's natural to you, or only a frontage for the bereavement you must feel?'

Rowan blinked hard. 'You mean you thought I'd be looking for a shoulder to cry on, and I'm not? Perhaps I could have done with one when Leone died—even yours or your father's. But nothing was on offer then—just silence. And as I can't bear women who make a profession of widowhood, embarrassing everybody about them, I'm not looking for that kind of sympathy any more,' she said tautly.

Another nod. 'Defiant words. You feel that our family failed you?'

'No more than it failed Leone when it cut him off and had nothing more to do with him because he wanted to be free to live his own life. I suppose I shouldn't have expected anything else. Even when he married me——'

'You judge us too harshly. I've explained why your letter wasn't answered at the time, but there was never any question that we should not get in touch with you ultimately.'

'Which I couldn't know, could I?' Rowan retorted.

'Unfortunately, no. But you have managed financially?'

'So far. I didn't give up my work as a school secretary when I married.'

'And Leone would have left you in funds.' Dario looked round the room. 'You wrote to us from this address. But when did you leave the one in Seymour Street?'

'*Seymour Street?*' Her echo was blank. 'I—we've never lived in Seymour Street! I know it. It's not far away. But it's all small shops, newsagents and grocers and so on——'

'But with apartments above them?'

'Perhaps—I've never looked to see. Why should you think we ever lived there?'

'Why? Because'—Dario took a paper from his wallet and consulted it—'number 18a Seymour Street, London N.W. is where we have regularly sent consignments of cash since Leone appealed for help from father soon after the birth of your child. As you must well know, *signora*,' he concluded.

'As *I* must know? Since——?' Empty echoes were all Rowan could manage as she fought for comprehension. 'I have no baby by Leone. We've never had one——'

'Never? It was about three years ago when you began to accept large amounts of money each month from my father—on behalf of Leone's son.'

'*No!*' she denied wildly. 'I know nothing of any money. Leone didn't write to his father, nor hear from any of your family—ever. And as for his having given me a son,'—she knew she had flushed an angry crimson as she faced her accuser—'I'd have thought that you, as his brother, would know that Leone—couldn't.'

She saw that he understood. 'My family thought we did,' he said. 'But perhaps a stigma like that must have an end, or at least a check in one generation, and on Leone's evidence it seemed it had.'

'And it hadn't. Leone confessed to me.' Rowan beat a desperate fist upon the arm of her chair. 'I have no——'

Dario had risen from his chair and was now standing over her. He had taken something else from his wallet and was putting his savage question, claiming proof he must think she was powerless to deny.

She had said nothing in reply to his sardonic invitation to tell the truth, and after a minute or two's silence, he went back to his seat, leaving the snapshot face upward on a low table between them. He seemed prepared to wait for her to begin, and after a time she did.

'Leone and I were not introduced,' she said. 'He was in front of me in a queue for tickets for *Rigoletto* at Covent Garden. He was the last person to get any, and he apologised charmingly for beating me to it. He offered me one of his, but I wouldn't take it. But we talked, and we did go to the opera later together. And to other places . . . until we were doing most things together and knew we were falling in love. We'd known each other about three months when we married.'

'You, knowing he believed he couldn't have children?' Dario asked.

Rowan shook her head. 'No, not then. I didn't know until I told him I wanted a baby. He told me then; he'd been afraid of losing me before, he said. That was much later.'

'And you believed him?'

She looked at Dario almost in pity of his obtuseness. 'Well, we had no children, did we?' she asked.

His finger stabbed towards the table. 'What about that? My father had that from Leone only a short while ago—a child with a name and a likely age——'

'*But no son of ours!* How often must I tell you? And do you suppose a doctor couldn't confirm that I've never had a child?' she demanded in desperation.

That seemed to count with him. He studied her face for so long that he outstared her angry eyes. Then he said, 'Very well. We'll go on from there. How long was it after Leone's admission, and whose idea was it, that you decided a fictitious son and heir should be good for extracting some funds from the Cortese family coffers? *Regular* funds, generous ones, paid monthly by banker's order. A minimum of correspondence, because you knew—rightly—that it wouldn't be answered. Just the announcement of a birth, a hint that the surprise breaking of the family stigma called for a rich endowment, and the later devilishly clever trick of a photograph showing a child of the right age—*any* child snapped at play on *any* beach and given a name, Scipio Cortese—If that was the way the plot really went, for God's sake, woman, admit it!'

Aghast, Rowan stammered, 'It wasn't. It wasn't! There was no plot!'

'First no child, then no plot. And no money passed either, I suppose?' Dario sneered.

'If—if it did, I didn't know.' While he had been talking, accusing, she had been forced to realise how near to the truth he was. *Leone.* There had been a plot and it had been Leone's. There could be no other reason for Dario's belief that she had a child than that Leone had let his father believe it, seeing the kudos to be gained from it and working on the details, even to the point of that bogus 'proof'. Knowing he dared not admit it to her, deceiving her in this as he had deceived her over his other secret—for years!

As if from a long way off she heard Dario question, 'You didn't know? I fail to see how that could be. Unless Leone was salting the money away privately, you must have realised the point in time at which your fortunes took a turn for the better?'

She had. 'But I thought—Leone told me—his dealing in cars was improving tremendously.'

'You shared bank accounts?'

'No. We each had our own. But after he died,

though he spent a lot—too much, I thought—there was more in his account than I expected.'

'How was that? You must surely have questioned and been told what this regular arrival of mail from Rome was about?' Dario paused. 'That is, unless you didn't need telling, because you had been in the plot from the beginning.'

Through set teeth she rasped, 'Which I wasn't. I've *told* you! And do you think I should have been surprised about Seymour Street, if Leone had ever told me he was using it as—what is it called?—an accommodation address?' (Surely he *must* see the logical argument of that?)

But Dario remained unmoved. 'Surprise can be simulated. And I simply do not accept that, for as close a couple as you seem to have been, you would not have been in his confidence in so big a thing as this. However——'

'You can't just leave it at "However"!'

'I can for the moment. I'd like to hear more now about the accident in which Leone was killed—your letter didn't give details.'

'It was heavily foggy. He was demonstrating a car to a client, when a car in trouble flagged them down to help to push it off the highway. Leone got out and was pushing, when a third car, travelling too fast, piled up on them, killing Leone instantly and injuring the other man. I thought you might at least have acknowledged my letter, but I didn't really expect it,' she finished hardly.

Dario said, 'I've explained why you weren't answered at the time, and my father, whose will is rarely questioned, only decided a few days ago to take you and your child into his care by bringing you both home to the Villa Cortese. That is why I am here—to fetch you.'

'To——?' Rowan gasped her dismay. 'That's impossible! You must go back without me.'

'So? I think not,' Dario drawled. 'You will come with me.'

'I can't! I have a job here.'

'You must leave it—sacrifice pay in lieu of notice.'

'I—— That is, I haven't a job for the moment. But——'

'Then there's no problem, is there?'

'No problem? No *problem*?' she almost shrilled. 'My father-in-law expects to welcome me and Leone's son, and you say there's no problem to presenting me to him—alone!'

'It is precisely because you *are* alone, with no son by Leone, that you *must* come. You understand why, I hope?' Dario insinuated.

She looked into his dark, hostile eyes and read no pity there. 'Yes, I understand,' she said slowly. 'You don't believe I wasn't in this with Leone for the money, and you'll speak no word for me to his father. I'm to escape no blame that's due to me. You're pretty sure I'll be doubted, and you'll lift not a finger to help. I'm to be out on my own, and I have to go to Rome with you, so that you can see it all happening. Isn't that what you hope I understand, *signore*?'

'Almost precisely,' he agreed. 'It's as well you appreciate that you must come. It saves my insisting that you plead your own case with my father, who isn't likely to be easily persuaded of your innocence in this.' As if satisfied he had concluded his business with her, Dario stood up, adding, 'And so I propose to give you, say, three days to make your arrangements here. Do you rent this apartment? You do? Then give notice of leaving it for an indefinite time. That will be taken care of. Are you in immediate need of money?'

'No.'

He put away the wallet he had produced. 'Then I shall book our flight for Friday, the noon plane from Heathrow. I shall call for you at ten. In the meantime this telephone number—my hotel—will reach me. *A rivederci, signora.*'

He did not wait to see the petty, futile gesture with which she tore in two the scribbled card he handed to her. He also left behind the photograph of the unknown child to mock her.

Hail had been dancing on the tarmac as they had boarded the aircraft. The Rome afternoon was a golden glow of light under a cloudless sky, and for all her despair Rowan felt her spirits lift slightly in face of such of the city's mellow beauty as she glimpsed on the drive from the airport to

the Villa Cortese. If things had been different, if
Leone had been other than he was, this might
have been *her* city, by courtesy of the Roman
family whose Rome it was and who would have
welcomed her to it, making her one of them.

She would have come here with Leone, a
daughter for the house which had none of its
own. For a brief euphoric moment or two she let
herself pretend that the finely-cut profile of the
man at her side *was* Leone's, so like was it to that
of the husband for whom she had wept too often,
at first in desolation at his loss, but now for the
false gallant and cheat he had been.

Or had her tears of the last three nights been
more for herself; tears of chagrin and anger
against Leone for putting her at the mercy of
Dario and his family from whom she could hope
for none? Whichever they had been, she had
steeled her will to shed no more. When she had
pleaded her case with the family she must go
away and put Leone behind her. Dario, for one,
would never let her be a Cortese of Rome. He
hadn't that much of charity in him.

He collected his long open car from the airport
car-park and drove north across the city, bridging
the Tiber in the working-class district of
Trastevere, pointing out the grandeur of the
famous monuments they passed and indicating
the rough direction of others—the Colosseum,
the ruins of the Forum, the Vatican, the Square
from which the Spanish Steps mounted to the

twin-cupolaed church above, which they skirted to enter the Villa Borghese Gardens, the largest park in Rome.

The expanse of its grass was immense, the green of its trees in young leaf was of a dozen different shades against the darker background of its conifers. Orchards and even vineyards divided it, and avenues bordered by blossoming magnolias and ilex trees criss-crossed it. A public boulevard crossed its northern boundary; here there were mansions, apart from each other by their private grounds. On the sweep of drive curving to one of these, its frontage full to a view of the Borghese park, Dario drew up. 'The Villa Cortese,' he said.

Not 'Here we are', nor even 'This is my home', but presenting it in the same tone of flat commentary he had used for the other sights of the city. Treating me as dutifully as he would a tourist on a whistle-stop round of Europe; knowing the cold welcome I shall get here, and warning me not to think of his home and Leone's as mine, thought Rowan on a stab of resentment. His manner had been just so on the flight out—scrupulously courteous and as glacial as black frost.

She looked up at the house. It was dazzlingly white, as even newly cleaned buildings in London never were. A stone-balustraded balcony ran the length of its façade at first-floor level; below were a row of deep windows, and above were three floors more. On each side it was flanked by long stone walls with the pointed tips of cypress trees showing above them. Determined not to show Dario her awe of it with any exclamation, she said flatly, 'It's a bigger house than I expected, but Leone had never told me much about it. Something of a "stately home", isn't it? Quite a showplace?'

She saw from Dario's quick frown that he had read the disparagement she had intended. But he countered with a shrug and a careless, 'Just a little nonsense thrown together by a former Pope and given to my family four centuries ago,' which left her feeling that he had won that round.

He pressed his horn twice before helping her out, and by the time they reached the portico to the front door, a manservant was opening to them and hustling a boy behind him to fetch their luggage from the car.

'Il maestro is expecting you,' he told Dario. 'He is in the studio.'

'Signora Lucia is with him?—My aunt,' Dario added in an aside to Rowan, who nodded. She knew that Arturo Cortese's spinster sister-in-law had kept house for him since his wife had died.

'No, he is alone,' said the man.

'Very well, Emilio, we'll go to him. Or no, here he is——' Dario broke off to go several paces down a corridor leading off the hall to meet the man coming slowly up it with the aid of an ebony stick. As he emerged into the sunlight of the hall Rowan saw that Arturo Cortese was tall, spade-bearded, his face and figure cast in the same handsome mould as his sons'. Leone was there in the shooting glance of his dark eyes, and Dario was there in the strong lines of his face, the proud carriage of his head.

He gave a hand to Dario and looked beyond him to Rowan. 'You are——?' he questioned.

She moved forward, her heart thudding in her throat. 'Rowan, *signore*,' she said simply. 'Leone's widow. You sent for me.'

'Ah. Rowan.' He pondered the name, then repeated it. 'Rowan,' and looked about him. 'And where is the child? He is with you? Your son, Leone's—S-Scipio?'

The tiny stammer over the name was the only warning to his hearers of what happened next— his frantic, white-knuckled clutch upon the walking stick, the uncontrolled crumpling of his face and his limbs' total collapse, his heavy fall to the marble floor broken only by Dario's swift move to catch him as he fell. Within the space of a minute his imperious figure had taken on the sad limpness of rag, his penetrating eyes were shuttered and he had become a sick man for Rowan's pity, no longer her fear.

As Dario laid his burden down, she plucked at his elbow. 'Is—is there anything I can do?' she asked. He ignored her to call to the departing Emilio, 'Bring blankets, pillows, and stay here while I ring the doctor.' Then he turned upon Rowan.

'No, nothing,' he told her curtly. 'This looks like his second stroke, and all one can do for the moment is to try to minimise the initial shock. No, efface yourself, please. Go and sit down— here.' He went with her to open a door to an elegant drawing-room, its curtains drawn against the sun. 'I'll have a maid sent to you to show you to your suite, and I'll bring you news of Father as soon as I can.'

He left her, and she sat on the edge of a Louis Quinze chair, waiting.

No hint of reassurance for *her* shock, she thought painfully. Could he have been so terse, so dismissing, if his subconscious weren't damning her with blame for her father-in-law's collapse at the very point of their meeting? He might not be aware of such thinking, or, knowing of it, might not admit it openly. But she was wretchedly convinced she had read the accusation in his eyes.

CHAPTER TWO

THE sun went down in a pink flamingo sky and Rowan was still waiting for Dario or someone to notice her existence after the maid he had summoned had left her.

It was indeed a 'suite' which had been prepared for her—an ornate, high-ceilinged room on the first floor, furnished as a boudoir with comfortable chairs, a writing desk, a television set—and two small bedrooms with a shower-room between them. The bed in one of these was only a cot under a Mickey Mouse coverlet to match the miniature cupboards with Mickey Mouse painted doors.

'For the little one,' the girl explained with well-trained lack of curiosity as to why there was no little one with Rowan, who conjectured wretchedly that unless the Cortese family was extremely discreet, it would not be long before its domestic staff knew why.

But by that time she would not be there to endure the shame of exposure. She hadn't any doubt of the seriousness of her father-in-law's collapse, and with his father too ill to see her, Dario would certainly be thankful to see the back of her as soon as she could leave. If he blamed her, as she was sure he did, he wouldn't risk another meeting between her and the Conte. If he came to see her as he had promised, he might let her go tonight, and with that hope in view she unpacked nothing but the air travel satchel containing her toilet things. The Rowan Cortese who would be going back to London was making no claim to even one night of the welcome that had been awaiting the widowed Rowan Cortese who was supposed to be the mother of Leone's child.

The deep window to the room gave on to the balustraded balcony she had seen from the car, and she was sitting at the window in the twilight, looking out over the darkening park, when at last Dario came to her. He flicked on lights as he entered, following his knock, and looked surprised to see her still wearing the tweed suit in which she had travelled from London.

'I'd have thought you'd be glad to change,' he said. 'Didn't Emilio bring up your cases?'

Rowan said, 'Your maid had them when she showed me up.' She gestured to the luggage stand near the door. 'But I didn't unpack because I thought that—now—you wouldn't want me to stay.'

'Stay?' Dario echoed. 'Of course you will stay. What do you mean?'

'Well—your father's illness. He can't see me, can he? And isn't that what you brought me for? To—to explain, and then leave?'

Dario's mouth pulled one-sidedly. '"Explain"—the understatement of the year!' he mocked, then mimicked savagely, '"Please, father-in-law, Leone and I played a trick on you, meaning no harm, though we *did* rather need the money. What I'm saying is, I haven't brought you a grandson; we never had one for you because Leone *couldn't* ... If that's all right by you, father-in-law dear——" Was that the way you meant it to go, before you bowed out, shriven of guilt, your conscience cleared by a little enforced flit to Rome and an "explanation"?' Dario paused and on a long-drawn breath added, 'If that's so, my dear sister-in-law, you were never more mistaken in your young life!'

Shuddering, Rowan covered her face with her hands. 'Don't!' she begged. 'You're cruel, you mean to hurt—deliberately!'

'To enforce a necessary point, yes, perhaps,' he agreed. 'In the name of clarity I can be as cruel as the next man. As you'll find if you persist in harbouring the idea that, having been spared your penitence piece this afternoon, you are free to slough it off for good and go your way, because someone else—I, for instance—will have to tell Father the truth when he is better and *can* hear it. In short, you needn't be there to face the consequences, and if that's the way your thinking goes, as I've warned you, you couldn't be more wrong.'

She lifted her head to stare at him. 'You mean

to keep me here until he *is* better, however long
that may be?'

'However long,' Dario confirmed. 'On the
evidence of his first attack, it isn't likely to be
mere days before he is in command again of his
speech, his hearing and the rest. Weeks, perhaps.
Or more probably, some months. Yes, you will
still be here. And something you may not have
fully understood is that, even if you had been
able to tell your story today, you would not have
been free to wash your hands of us and leave.
You would have stayed to learn and to live with
what you and Leone had done to shame our
family for as long as we see fit that you should
stay. It could, you know, be quite a time before
we throw you out.'

'You can't keep me here against my will!'
Rowan flared at that.

'If not, we shall have to see that your
conscience can, shan't we?'

'This isn't even your house!'

'True, but I think you'll find that everyone in
it will be of the same mind about your immediate
future. Meanwhile you will not be embarrassed
outside it. It is not the Roman way to air family
skeletons in the open, and no one but Zia
Lucia—your aunt-in-law, my father and I, know
that we were expecting to welcome Leone's
widow and his son today. By my father's wish,
Leone's name has hardly been mentioned in
public since he first left Rome, and few people

will have heard of your widowhood, until we choose to tell them who you are. If you are asked about children, you yourself can tell the truth—that you have none,' Dario concluded.

'You should have told the Conte the truth before you brought me here,' Rowan accused.

'How? By telephone? By letter? How do you suppose the news would have read? Besides, you'd have been spared an ordeal I considered you had earned.'

'*But* spared him the shock of finding I'd come alone! Because you're blaming me for his attack this afternoon. Aren't you? I know it,' she claimed.

He spread an expressive hand. 'With reservations. When a patient has had one major stroke, it is always on the cards he may have another.'

'Thank you. Thank you *very* much for the benefit of the doubt,' she sneered, adding, 'Do I take it that Signora—your aunt—does know now that I came alone, and why?'

'Signora Battisto,' Dario supplied. 'My aunt on my late mother's side. Yes, I have told her why I brought you. She had to know.'

'And——?'

'Her reaction was——' he paused as if to choose a word—'understandable. But you will meet her at dinner.'

'*If* I am at dinner myself!' But Rowan knew it was a futile defiance, a weak stand against this man's determination to show her no quarter. Yet,

awed as she was by the strength of his will, she
felt a reluctant respect for his power. To beat in
vain against such a wall of tenacity was a new
experience for her; by contrast Leone had been as
amiably pliant as soft clay; going along with her,
even while, as she knew now, he had been her
secret enemy. There was nothing secret about
Dario Cortese's enmity; it was as inflexible as
stone, and there was challenge in the very
obduracy of stone . . .

'You will be there,' he said with cool assurance.
'Later we must discuss with Zia Lucia the
arrangements for your stay. For instance, you
would like the nursery bedroom dismantled, and
your personal allowance defined? Other things—a
maid, if you want one——'

'A personal allowance?' Rowan's understanding
had caught up slowly. 'You mean money? I don't
want it. I wouldn't take any from you! I have
funds——'

'Enough—for your position here as Leone's
widow? I think probably not,' Dario decided.
'The amount I know my father planned for you
will be put into the bank of your choice for your
use while you are here.'

It occurred to her to remind him that she had
been considered worthy of no such bounty while
she had been Leone's wife. She might not have
existed until Leone had led them to believe she
had borne a male heir to their vaunted line. But
she compromised with a 'Do that with money if

you must. But I won't spend it.' To which he retorted, 'If you won't, then it will be spent for you. In fact'—during a long disconcerting pause his study of her figure was an insolent appraisal of her as a woman—'I might be tempted to dress you myself, and it would be a pity if our tastes didn't coincide.'

Both look and taunt were a first sign of his personal awareness of her, and she despised the surge of flame to her face. At a loss for a telling retort, she attempted none and changed the subject with the belated question, 'How is your father? Must he go to hospital?'

'No. He will be professionally nursed, night and day, in his own suite in the east wing, as he was in the autumn. At present he will be allowed no visitors except Zia Lucia and myself.'

'Does he remember that I am here?' Rowan asked.

'If he does, he can't communicate as much yet. But don't count on his never regaining his memory or his speech as your easy way out,' Dario warned coldly.

Rowan flushed again, this time in a swift burn of anger. 'How dare you suggest I could be hoping he might never recover his faculties, or that he might die?' she demanded.

'Dare *you* suggest the thought never crossed your mind?' Dario countered.

'I can!'

He shook his head. 'I don't believe you. You

wouldn't be human if, when you saw him collapse, you didn't thank Providence for being on your side.'

'Then I'm not human!' she declared wildly.

'But still humanly craven enough to cash in on the respite you'd gained. A quarter of an hour ago didn't I find you poised for flight, running away while there was still time?' He paused. 'Or could I be wrong and you were making a bid to escape from *me*, seeing my father as the lesser threat to you of two?'

She hated his diabolical insight with which he had pinpointed the truth—that she hadn't been fleeing the Conte's as yet unspoken wrath as she had been running before the present storm of his son's cruel prejudice and contempt. But she wouldn't let him know it. 'If I'd been afraid of you, should I have come with you at all?' she flung at him.

'You could hardly do otherwise, in the face of your guilt.'

'Guilt I don't admit to, except of allowing Leone to deceive me. But if I'd refused to come, you could hardly have used physical force. Or might you have tried it?' she defied him.

He shrugged. 'The crude force of shipping you, bound hand and foot and gagged—no. But I'd remind you there are subtler physical means open to a man of persuading a woman against her will.'

She didn't understand him. 'Physical means—such as?' she queried.

He turned to the door. 'Think of a few, and choose the one which is popularly supposed to humiliate your sex most,' he advised—and left her.

Furious that her naïve question had actually asked for that insult, the meaning of which he must know she would understand very well, Rowan despaired of forgetting it unless she could plan some counter-move which might help to close her mind against it.

Rape—or something approaching it. He wouldn't dare . . . would he? No, she must *not* remember he had threatened it. She must think of something else, do something active . . . shut out the thought of exploratory hands, enforcing arms, lips lustful and demanding, body—Dario Cortese's body—taking its cruel toll for revenge's sake . . . It was a dark image which she had to put behind her, *had* to!

One positive thing she could not do now was to escape him physically by leaving. It would be so easy. She had only to pick up her bags, walk out of this room and out of the house, find herself a taxi and go. But she wouldn't do it. Dario had been more cunning than perhaps he knew when he had suggested her conscience would hold her back from attempting escape that way. For something—conscience, challenge or just plain bravado—would keep her here in face of whatever lay ahead.

Admitting this, deciding it, helped. She turned to the mundane task of unpacking her things and putting them away, noticing in the long wardrobe mirror how unsuitably she was dressed for a warm Roman evening. But what *was* suitable for dining with the enemy? She chose and laid out a ballet-length black crêpe with batwing sleeves and a high neckline, and was taking a bath when the idea occurred to her of trying to meet her hostess before she had to do so at dinner with Dario, saturnine and withdrawn, looking on.

Would she risk the snub of all time if she dared ask for an audience of Leone's Zia Lucia, of whom he had given her no mental picture at all? (Strange, how little Leone had ever talked of his family, as if he had counted them out of his life. Until of course he had decided to *use* them ... But that was another ugly thought on which she must shut her eyes.)

She rang the bell the maid had pointed out to her ('It sounds in the kitchen parts. Someone will come'), and presently someone, the same girl, did. Rowan had prepared her question. 'Do you think Signora Battisto could see me some time before dinner, if she is free?'

'But of course, *signora*. This hour of the evening she rests in her room. I will show you the way,' the girl offered. As she led Rowan along a marble-floored corridor strewn with Persian rugs, she pointed to closed doors—'Signor

Dario's room and study', next beyond Rowan's
suite; 'the married guests' apartment' and beyond
that, 'the room of the Signora,' all facing, like
Rowan's, outward to the Borghese Gardens.

'*Grazie*.' Rowan thanked the girl, knocked and
went in, obeying the summons, '*Entra*,' which
answered her knock. The woman who turned
from a writing desk was white-haired with a
strongly lined face, lean corded neck and a spare
figure clad in a rather shapeless dress of flowered
material. She drew a shawl about her shoulders as
she stood with the aid of a stick like her brother-
in-law's. Rowan stood speechless before her, not
knowing how to introduce herself nor what her
reception would be. She had to face the scrutiny
of sharp dark eyes for a long minute until Lucia
Battisto pointed imperiously to a chair and
ordered in Italian, 'Sit down, please, *mia nipote*.
You bring us bad news and, Dario thinks, may
have caused us some more with Arturo's shock
and collapse. But perhaps Dario is wrong about
that, and we have to blame you only for your part
in Leone's cruel deception of his father over the
years, which is quite enough for you to explain
and justify to us—not so?'

Rowan agreed, 'More than enough, *signora*——'

'Zia Lucia. You are Leone's widow.'

'Zia Lucia.' Rowan had been encouraged by
being called 'my niece', but that hadn't spared
her the harsh criticism which had followed,
qualifying the familiarity. Clearly Dario had got

in first with his denunciation of her and had been
believed. She could expect little mercy here
either. She said again, 'More than enough——'
and suddenly deciding that as she had already
been prejudged, she hadn't much to lose by
shouldering Leone's guilt, added, 'That was
unforgivable, I know.'

'Not only unforgivable—rash to a degree!
Sooner or later Arturo would have expected to
meet a grandson, as he did when he sent Dario to
England, and what would Leone have done about
your secret then?' Lucia's deep contralto voice
demanded.

It was a question about the future which even
Dario hadn't asked, and as it had never been her
secret to hide, Rowan could only reply with a
blank, 'I don't know.'

'You don't know,' Lucia echoed flatly. 'And
nor, I'd hazard, did Leone, in his conceit as a fool
turned knave who thinks he needn't look ahead.
He was fortunate, was he not, that he was able to
leave you to confess the truth?'

'If to be dead as he died, helping someone else,
is "fortunate",' Rowan murmured quietly, 'yes.'

There was a moment's silence. Then, less
harshly, 'You loved him, did you?' Lucia asked.

There had once been a Leone whom she could
love and did. 'Yes,' Rowan said truthfully of that
Leone, bidding it farewell as she spoke.

Lucia had turned back to her desk, squaring its
blotter, sheathing her fountain pen. Speaking to

them, rather than to Rowan, she said, 'And so, the family is left with the consequences of your lies, and you with their guilt which you will have to confess to Arturo when he recovers. One cannot know how much he may have guessed before he collapsed, but you must stay here until he can understand what you have to tell him.'

Rowan said, 'Yes, so Dario has insisted, though I wonder if he realises how difficult that will be for me.'

'Difficult?'

'Embarrassing for us all, surely?'

Lucia turned about. 'That is something you have brought on us, but Dario and I can rise above it, and you must do the same. By reason of your marriage you are a daughter in my brother's house, and it is not the Cortese habit to harass their own kind; this matter will not be held against you while you are our guest.' She paused. Then, 'I am glad you came to see me, niece, enabling us to introduce ourselves before your first meal in Arturo's house, at which, I assure you, our talk will be of other things.' She looked at her watch. 'Now I must dress. Ask Maria to show you to the small *sala da pranzo* where we eat when we are alone.'

Rowan thanked her and left. The encounter had solved nothing, and the chilly distance at which Lucia kept her was daunting to any appeal for understanding of her innocence. In fact she realised that she herself had allowed the older woman to believe her as guilty as Leone. She supposed she must be grateful to the 'Cortese habit' for the assurance that she would be treated as a guest, rather than as a prisoner on remand.

She did not trouble the maid again but found the small dining-room herself.

There was something unreal about a meal at which three people studiedly avoided discussion of a subject which must be uppermost in their minds. But Rowan concluded the tension must be all hers, for neither Dario nor Lucia gave any sign of it. The food—a consommé, duckling breasts in a sour-sweet sauce, followed by candied strawberries—was impeccably cooked and served, and though she had only a nervous appetite for it, she concentrated on it in silence, leaving the other two to talk.

Before dinner Dario had visited his father's sickroom and reported on his condition to Lucia, who worried aloud that his hastily summoned nurses shouldn't have all they needed for his care. Dario reassured her. The day nurse had gone off duty and the night nurse had taken over; Arturo was sleeping under sedation and the doctor would make another call before midnight.

Then, incredibly to Rowan, they were discussing her entertainment. She did not know Rome? Then she must be shown all its famous sights—its churches, its squares, its ruins, its ancient Appian Way, its legendary fountains, its streets

of de luxe shops. Who, they debated, could act as
her guide? Who, Lucia suggested, but Andrea
Bellini? Andrea frequently complained of having
time on her hands. Her husband Biron was too
often away from home. She was bored and idle
and knew everyone in Rome. Who better then
than Andrea to introduce it to Rowan?

This apparent detachment from their own
problems and hers Rowan found amazing until
she realised that it was probably in their own
interests to keep up the fiction of her having been
invited to the Villa only as Leone's widow;
belatedly cherished after Leone's long estrange-
ment, to which, Dario had said, they never
referred, nor told their friends the news from
Leone that Rowan had borne him a child. This
spared their having to explain the absence or
death of a child about whom people might
enquire. They had kept their secret until now, so
hadn't now to admit to Leone's lies and
extortions, and tonight, Rowan's instinct told
her, Dario and Lucia were conducting a private
rehearsal of the situation they would show to
their public—the proud Cortese family cupboard
closing doors upon the rattle of bones inside!

As they talked, assuming her compliance with
their plans, a name touched a chord in Rowan's
memory. Andrea. A cousin Andrea Vancusa
whom Dario had wanted to marry, Leone had
said but who had married someone else. Andrea
Bellini now, with a husband Biron of that name,

Rowan supposed, wondering why she found it difficult to think of Dario in love and losing out to another man. Dario, she would have said, was one of the winners of this world by sheer force of a character to which people did not say No . . .

Lucia was explaining Andrea Bellini now. 'She is Dario's and Leone's cousin, my niece by my younger sister, Margharita. Her husband, Biron, breeds thoroughbred horses. They have a villa on the New Appian Way, and she is of about your age, I should think.'

'Rather older, surely?' Dario queried. 'Andrea is twenty-eight.' He turned to Rowan. 'And you, I think would not be that?'

'I am, just twenty-four,' she told him.

For their coffee they moved to a drawing-room furnished with antique chairs upholstered in old gold silk, matching the window curtains of rich brocade. On an occasional table near Rowan's chair were some glossy magazines, and, still more or less excluded from the small talk, she picked up one and was leafing through its pages when Lucia asked, 'Do you read Italian as well as you speak it?'

'A little better, I think. It's too easy to get out of practice when you are neither hearing it nor needing to speak it,' said Rowan.

Lucia nodded. 'Naturally. But here you will be able to speak it every day, and Dario, who is fluent himself in English, will keep you in practice in that. Yes, Dario?' she looked up at him as he joined them and took his coffee from her. 'You have rung Andrea and she will come over?'

'Yes—tomorrow. I invited her to luncheon. Was that all right? Biron is away.'

'As usual,' Lucia muttered cryptically. To Dario she added, 'You will be here?'

'No. After going to England I must have a long day at the office, and I can snatch a coffee and a *prosciutto* roll there.'

'Raw ham and black coffee—ruin to your digestion,' Lucia grumbled, but did not press him further. 'Dario must show you over the offices of Cortese Estates one day. They are on the Via Nationale and are rather fine,' she told Rowan, who wondered how long she and Dario could keep up this façade of cordial host and hostesship towards her. For it had to be an assumed frontage; in London Dario had made no secret of his distrust and hostility, so why had she to believe Lucia that in Rome their vaunted 'Cortese habit' would ensure his courtesy there? She, their guest indeed! How could they pretend it was so? What lay behind it all? And when they had done with pretending, what form would their snarling bitterness take?

She longed to escape, but knew that good manners demanded she must wait for Lucia's sign that she was free. At last it came. Lucia put away her needlepoint embroidery in a tapestry bag and stood up with an unsmiling '*Buona notte*' which Dario turned into 'Goodnight' as he went to open the door for Rowan. And how thankful they must be to wash off their greasepaint and be themselves for the space of a night, she thought rebelliously as she went up to her room.

She found that while she had been away the nursery bedroom had undergone a change. The cot was gone and so were the Mickey Mouse cupboards. Easy chairs and a music centre on a table had taken their place. Number one of Dario's 'arrangements' for her comfort! Would the next be an allotment of the money he had threatened to spend for her, if she wouldn't spend it herself?

Let him try! Just let him *try* to 'dress' her as he had warned he would. She shivered involuntarily. The look he had given her as he had spoken had seemed to strip her down to nudity while it lasted. He might once have suffered a calf love for his cousin Andrea and might not have married yet, but the Dario of that look *knew* women, she was convinced. It had no part in the debonair, detached Dario of this evening's farce. Whose fool did he think she was?

She had hardly expected to sleep, and she could not. The roar of the city was muted here to a continuous hum to which it was impossible not to listen and to wonder at what late or early morning hour it might cease. But even it was less of a disturbance than the tumult of her thoughts, and at last she had to escape them by some action. She switched on the light, pulled on her robe and slippers and went over to the deep window which she knew gave on to the long stone balcony. If Rome was still as wide awake as its noise indicated there should be something to see of its brilliance, if only a reflected glow in the night sky.

There was more, she discovered, stepping over the window lintel and going over to the stone balustrade. The lamps of the Gardens lighted the near-distance of the lawns and avenues, and to the south was spread a panorama of the city, its lighted streets and boulevards like jewelled snakes, the windows of its dark buildings winking and twinkling with lights of every colour in the spectrum.

The night air was very warm and Rowan lingered, arms akimbo on the balustrade, staring. Already she felt she could be taken by the magic of Rome. When she went back to bed she would try to concentrate on it, perhaps make plans to come back to it when this present nightmare was over, when she would still be a Cortese, but free.

She turned—and collided with one of the big stone vases lining the balcony. Empty as yet of its summer plantings, it was light enough to tip, and her reach to save its fall brought it back to base with a loud thump of stone on stone.

Rowan waited. Had it been heard? No, thank goodness. But as she froze, still holding its rim, a light came on in the next window along from her

own—Dario's apartment, Maria had said of it—
and Dario, still fully dressed, stepped out and
came over to her.

'What's the matter?' he asked.

'Nothing. I—I'm sorry.' She straightened. 'It
was this thing. I nearly knocked it over, and only
just caught it.'

'And——?' he invited, as if he hadn't the whole
story. So she gave it to him.

'I hadn't been able to sleep and I'd come out to
see what the city looked like by night.'

He turned at her side and looked out over the
balustrade. 'And how did you find it?'

She thought for a moment. 'Rather fine . . .
exciting.'

'Romulus and Remus did a good job, you
consider?'

'*And* the quacking geese who saved the Capitol
from the barbarians,' she capped his question.

'They too,' he agreed. 'Who taught you your
Roman legends? Leone?' he asked.

'No. I suppose I heard them along with fairy
tales. Leone hardly ever talked about Rome.'

'He never had any feelings for it. Nor for any
of his family—until he saw how to make use of
us. You must have been gratified by the length of
time we allowed your fiction to roll, weren't you?'

If he thought he could goad her into confessing
she had anything to do with it! She would *not*.
Nor plead her innocence again. 'You could have
exploded it any time earlier than you did,' she

reminded him. 'Why leave all sight of a baby the
Conte couldn't have expected me to have, until it
was—or would have been—three years old?'

'A good question with a simple answer,' Dario
allowed. 'Our family pride at work. Leone had
been cut off, and that went for you and your child
as well, until Leone was dead and my father had
himself looked death in the face with his first
stroke. Then I think he decided he could claim
the only heir he was likely to have, without loss of
face, and sent me for you—with what result you
know.'

'And you yourself? You were convinced too
that there was such a child as Scipio?' Rowan
questioned.

'Entirely. And hoped so equally with him.'

'And yet——' She checked and shook her head.
'Something I don't understand—you're as embit-
tered and intolerant as you've a right to be, and as
the Conte must be when he recovers. You
brought me here, meaning to make me confess to
him, and intending now to keep me here until I
can. And yet tonight you and your aunt treated
me just like your guest, someone you *wanted* to
please and entertain—Why?'

'We have to live with you, haven't we?' Dario
countered. 'Feed you? Fill your time?'

'You don't have to!'

'Nonsense. Our domestics and our friends
must accept you at the face value we give you—as
our guest and as Leone's childless widow to

whom we have long overdue family obligations and are fulfilling them as your due.'

'Than which nothing could be farther from the truth, could it?'

'But statecraft for which you should be grateful to us,' he shrugged.

'For lies told and acted on my behalf—*grateful*?' Rowan scorned.

'No lying called for. Simply a pleasant embroidery of the truth for public consumption and your ease with people. Doesn't that justify a bit of artifice? Though if your conscience is belatedly looking for a hair shirt, I daresay I could supply it with some rough stuff in private.' He paused, frowning at her. 'Or am I wrong, and it isn't your conscience that's troubling you, but your libido? In a virtuous widow desire has to go unsatisfied, I know, and I'm wondering whether, under that boyish golden thatch and fair English complexion, there might be a tougher skin with a dark, primitive need to be punished, to be hurt ... misused. There are such women who are perverse enough to enjoy martrydom with a kind of twisted pleasure. Are you one of them, I ask myself? Shall we see?'

She shrank from him, horrified and afraid. But his arms came to pinion her at the waist and a hand clamped cruelly over the swell of her breast.

'How—how——?' she panted. 'Let me *go*!' But he was pressing her back against the balustrade, the weight of his lean hard body holding her there. There was a black glitter in the eyes which met her panic-stricken gaze and an unspoken contempt in his scrutiny of her face before he kissed her with studied deliberation, forcing her lips apart with the brutish pressure of his own.

There was no response to him there. How could there be to the mimicry of a caress intended to diminish her, to punish? She struggled against steel without avail; her fists beat in vain until they were stilled by an even closer crush of his body to hers. His hands were now on her hips, arching her towards him in a physical contact with a man which she had not known for many long months. There was pain to it, and shame, and a terrible excitement of a wanting, a need, which were torture in themselves.

She could not have fought free if he hadn't suddenly released her and stood back.

'And what did you achieve by that?' she demanded in a strangled voice. 'Did you "see" the kind of woman I am—or not?'

'Up to a point,' he drawled.

'*What* point?'

'Where you showed that you do come in two layers—an outraged frigidity on top and a latent sensuality which you deny underneath. What, if anything new, did you learn about me?'

'Nothing more than that you're an opportunist as well as a sadist, and most decent people despise both,' she flung at him.

'Using the same measuring rod as for liars and

cheats. Frankly, would you say that in the matter of moral tarnish, there's much to choose between us?' he retorted.

She turned away and did not answer him, as he must have known she would not.

CHAPTER THREE

THOUGH she had told Dario she despised him, Rowan felt besmirched herself by that unbidden thrill of her flesh to his calculated manhandling of her body. After six months alone, was she so hungry for compelling arms about her that her senses had to betray her into desire at *this* man's contemptuous usage of her?

Her total reason protested that it wasn't so. Her readiness to melt must have been for Leone, mustn't it? It wasn't possible that some urge within her had wanted to respond to the hard mastery of his brother's hands and lips . . . Not possible at all.

She mustn't dwell on it, must forget Dario's callous assault had happened. She had to live with him and Lucia in the scenario they had devised for her, and tonight's raw exchange of insults fitted nowhere into that. Tomorrow, she supposed, they would be back on the impersonal level of guest and hosts—all for the saving of the Cortese 'face'.

Meanwhile, until she fell asleep at last, she puzzled over Dario's claim that with the news of Leone's death, the Conte had lost his hope of a grandson. But if the grim family tradition ran true, the birth of a son to Leone would surely have been an unlooked-for bonus. He must always have hoped for an heir through Dario, for whom there was no such blot on the escutcheon as there had been for Leone. The Conte himself had been a second son to his father, and *his* wife had borne him Leone and Dario, so why despair, before Dario had yet married, of the Cortese line's continuing to flourish through him and the wife he chose? What, if anything, did the Conte know of Dario's past or present which would leave him utterly without hope when the time came for Rowan herself to have to confess to him that there never had been a grandson for him through Leone? *What did Dario himself know, that he hadn't afforded his father at least some hope?* The problem followed Rowan into her uneasy dreams.

In the morning she found she was to breakfast alone on rolls and local honey and coffee. The maid who served her said Dario had left the Villa early after visiting the Conte's suite, and the Signora hoped Rowan would excuse her as she would take coffee in her room before going to sit with the Conte, to free the night nurse to take some exercise and the day nurse to have breakfast. The girl knew that Signora Bellini was expected in mid-morning, and suggested shyly that until she came, Signora Cortese might care to walk in the gardens.

Signora Cortese did care. The velvet lawns

invited and the great trees beckoned. There were shadowed avenues and hidden corners, and a formal Italian garden, all geometrically square and diamond and crescent-shaped flower beds, massed in spring colour and bordered by dwarf box and lavender.

There was a swimming pool surrounded by a glass-roofed piazza, and water steps and a fountain in full scintillating play into a basin with a centrepiece of grouped angels and horned devils in a stone-fixed harmony of their own.

Rowan sat here on the coping, watching and hearing the splash and tinkle of the falling water, and wondering how Leone had brought himself to leave such a place which would have been his own one day. Last evening she had belittled the house in order to score off Dario. But her scorn, which hadn't impressed him, had been assumed. She had recognised then, and even more so now, the value such a home must have for a family which had lived in it and cherished it for centuries.

A maroon sports car was parked on the drive when she returned to the house, and Lucia was greeting her niece in the hall. 'Ah, I had just sent to find you,' she told Rowan. 'Andrea arrived a few minutes ago. Andrea, *cara*—Leone's widow, Rowan,' she introduced them. 'Arturo wanted her to come to us, but as Dario will have told you, they had hardly met when he collapsed, so she has had a sad welcome, and we are glad you

will give her some of your time to entertain her.
She speaks Italian like one of us.'

'You do?' Andrea offered a slim hand to
Rowan. 'But of course—Leone. We were so
sorry, *signora*, when we heard——'

'Thank you. Losing him was a great shock,'
said Rowan, taking her cue in her role as a
blameless young widow whose arrival at the home
of her in-laws had been to 'a sad welcome.' As
Andrea turned to Lucia to ask about the Conte,
Rowan studied the looks of the woman who had
rejected Dario Cortese to marry elsewhere.

At twenty-eight Andrea Bellini had a narrow
graceful figure, its contours emphasised today by
tailored slacks and close-hugging sweater. Her
colouring was no acquired tan; it was a naturally
rich olive and she wore only eye make-up for the
rare green of her eyes. Her hair was a heavy black
spill to her shoulders; her classic profile was
marred only by the line of her mouth, sullen and
full-lipped almost to a pout of discontent. And
she had no repose, Rowan decided, watching the
repeated movement of her hand to maintain the
sweep of her hair over one eye, and the
gesticulation as she talked which kept the half-
dozen thin gold bracelets at her wrist to a
continuous jangle. She used both mannerisms to
effect. There was something seductive to that
loose outward turn of the wrist which set the
bracelets tumbling, and to the eye half shadowed
by the veil of hair. Had either or both been an

attraction for Dario? Rowan wondered. Or, when he had courted her as a girl in her early twenties, wasn't she then the poised, aware Andrea Bellini that marriage had made of her now?

Andrea was assuming, 'I may call you Rowan?' and making plans for their morning together. 'I have some shopping to do on the Via Condotti—that is one of our wealthiest streets. You will have seen the Spanish Steps on your way here? Last evening? Ah, well, the hippies and the flower-sellers would have gone home by then. And then we'll go for coffee on the Via Veneto—where everyone must be seen sooner or later.'

She and Lucia kissed each other's cheeks. Andrea promised to be back for lunch, but the full lips made a pronounced pout when she heard Dario would not be present.

'My husband makes a grass widow of me, and his friends avoid me,' she declared, though not as if she expected to be believed.

She was a skilled but daring driver, talking all the while as she threaded through the city morning traffic and joining in the raucous chorus of car horns with cheeky blasts on her own. She even managed to edge into a parking slot exactly opposite to the jewellers' shop she said she needed.

'I always exact a forfeit whenever Biron leaves me. That way I've built up quite a jewel-case, as he goes away pretty often,' she claimed to Rowan, as she told the bowing assistant who met them that she wanted to be shown bracelets. She chose another narrow one which went to join the others on her wrist; without asking its price she signed a chit for it, and then said she needed lingerie. She had so *much* crêpe-de-chine, and didn't Rowan agree that the very latest thing was lawn?

After that she shopped for crystal ware and sandals and a pair of antique candlesticks, paying in cash for nothing and ordering everything to be delivered. At the end of a very expensive morning Rowan felt it might equally have been spent in Bond Street as in exotic Rome. She hoped that Andrea, on any future guided trips, would take her farther afield than this, then made up for this ingratitude by buying Andrea a posy of rosebuds from a flower-girl on the Spanish Steps. Andrea murmured, 'Sweet of you, *cara*,' but had no pin with which to fasten them to her sweater, and left them in the glove compartment when she parked on Via Veneto.

There, over *capuccinos* and ice-cream, between waving to friends and pointing out film stars to Rowan, she asked a lot of questions and became confidential.

How long was Rowan staying in Rome? Had she had to leave a job to come over? Had Leone been able to leave her comfortable, money-wise? Perhaps it was too early to ask, but would Rowan think of marrying again? And how did she like her in-laws, Dario and Zia Lucia and the little she had seen of the Conte, poor man?

'Before I married Biron Bellini, Dario made a long play for me,' Andrea reminisced. 'That was five or six years ago, and I did think of taking him—he is so *male*, and he was utterly besotted over me. But I met Biron at a party and somehow said Yes to him instead. Since when Dario hasn't looked at another woman seriously, one hears.'

'After five or six years?' Rowan doubted a little cynically.

Andrea's hand gestured gracefully. 'I said *seriously*. You must know what I mean. Of course there have been women for him—of a sort. But only for—use, if I make myself clear?'

First finding out what kind they are, and punishing them for not being what he wants, thought Rowan, remembering last night. She nodded Yes to Andrea, who sat forward to the café table, chin resting in her hand. 'You know, I do wonder,' she mused, 'whether I should have married Dario when he wanted me to. After all, there's nothing about *his* being unable to have children, as there was with Leone—oh, I'm sorry——' she broke off at Rowan's movement of recoil, then went on, 'But you did know about that? It's something that has always been known about the Cortese line, and Leone must have told you before you married him?'

'Yes, I knew,' Rowan admitted. It was no business of Andrea's that she had learnt the truth too late.

'Too bad, if you'd have liked children.' Andrea

went on, 'I don't know if I would or not. They
could be a bore and they do *age* a woman. But a
sign of my need of them—which is different from
wanting, isn't it?—is my urge to spend, spend, up
to the hilt, so my analyst says.'

'Your analyst?'

'Yes, I see him once a week; he claims to know
more about me than I do myself. Which reminds
me—he is taking me out to dinner tonight. Why
don't we make a foursome of it, with Dario as the
man for you?'

Rowan had her doubts as to whether Dario's
show of hospitality to her went as far as being
partnered with her for dining out. 'I don't
think——' she began. But Andrea, calling their
waiter, wasn't listening. On their way back to the
Villa, she said, 'I'll ring Dario from home at his
office. After escaping me for lunch, he won't dare
say No.'

Nor, to Rowan's intense surprise, had Dario
apparently said No. She had thought he might
plead concern for his father if he didn't care to
admit he had no intention of escorting her. He
had only to claim that the emergency of the
Conte's condition must keep him on hand that
evening. After that raw scene on the balcony last
night, how would he behave to her tonight? How
did he expect *her* to ignore all memory of it? She
hadn't learnt her new part well enough to pretend
it hadn't happened! And yet when he rang the
Villa at six to ask that she be ready to leave with

him for the restaurant at eight, she didn't send
back the maid with a refusal. The challenge of the
man's effect upon her still rankled, and she had to
meet it head-on. Besides, she felt a certain
curiosity to see him and Andrea—the jilt and the
jilted,—together.

As she changed into the other one of the two
dinner dresses she owned—the black batwing last
night, the celadon green princess line this—she
remembered Dario's gibe about dressing her
himself. She hadn't known, when she had packed
in London, that she would be a prisoner of the
Cortese household for longer than it would take
for her to arrive, to make her confession to the
Conte and be thrown out. Three days, perhaps
only two. She mightn't even have been asked to
change her clothes at all! But tomorrow, if she
were to continue to play in the grim charade, she
must go and buy some. *Not*, however, on the Via
Condotti. There must be a Roman Oxford Street
or Kensington High Street *somewhere*!

She supposed she might have known Dario
would show no embarrassment when they met. His
hostility was evidently for private usage between
them, not to be indulged, even before Lucia.

In the car on their way to the restaurant he
reverted to the subject of an allowance for her. 'I
have opened an account for you at my own bank,
the Nationale. Zia will go with you tomorrow for
you to give the necessary signatures and collect
your cheque book,' he said.

Rowan's hackles rose. 'I told you I wouldn't accept money from you!' she defied.

'And I'm only carrying out your father-in-law's wish to provide you with funds. I've not gone to the trouble to provide you with references and to transfer money to you, for the account to lie unused. You didn't bring much luggage with you, and you will need more in your wardrobe for a Roman summer than for one in London.'

'Taking for granted that I shall be *here* for the summer?'

'Providing for the probability that you may be,' he replied coolly. 'Andrea will advise you on where to shop, I'm sure.'

'Thank you, but for whatever I need to buy—and I have some money of my own—I shall have to go to shops I can afford. I went shopping with your cousin this morning, and I'm afraid I can't compete.'

He threw a swift glance her way, then looked front again into the traffic. 'Few women in her circle can,' he said dismissingly, making her blush for the simplicity of the green dress and the light stole on her shoulders, which hadn't made the grade with the criticism in his glance. He had measured her by the yardstick of Andrea Bellini's chic, and found her wanting. Well, all right, she wasn't in Andrea's league. But he needn't make it quite so obvious—need he?

Andrea and her escort, introduced as Dr Martius

Guardia, a bearded blond, were at the restaurant before them. Andrea, in scarlet wool, side-slashed to her knee and the black hair piled to the crown of her head, kissed Dario in greeting. 'There aren't many men I allow to cut lunching with me,' she sparkled at him. 'What did you mean by it, *caro mio*? Your excuse had better be good!'

'Any reason I give you, you would shred to pieces, so I won't go to the trouble of offering you one,' he told her. 'When is Biron coming home?'

'Tomorrow.'

'Then you won't be free to give your time to taking Rowan about?'

'Why not? Perhaps not tomorrow, when I must lay on a welcome for my lord. But after that, his being at home or away makes little difference to *my* time. Showing Rowan the sights will make a nice change from sitting around, waiting for a smoke signal that there will be a party of eight or ten or whatever for dinner, or that I'm free to dine from a tray in front of the television, because he will be eating out.'

There was no mistaking the bitterness in Andrea's tone, and Rowan wondered if the two men were as embarrassed as she. But Dario ignored Andrea's washing of the linen of her marriage in public to suggest, 'Rowan would like to do some shopping, and would appreciate your advice on where to go.' Upon which Andrea brightened at once.

'But of course,' she agreed eagerly. 'What are you looking for in particular?' she asked Rowan. 'Clothes? Shoes? We must make a date.'

Over dinner the talk was mostly of local events and of personalities Rowan did not know. She was the outsider, looking on, seeing Andrea and Dario together, but learning very little, from her provocative banter and his enigmatic fencing, of what their present relationship was. Dr Guardia's role, Rowan felt, was rather that of the proud parent of a precocious child—Andrea—who was showing off. He 'fed' her with lines and laughed too readily when she capped them.

As they were leaving Andrea had a suggestion. 'Why don't we go slumming in the Trastavere? There is sure to be an all-night market going, and we can park the cars at the Portese Gate. Let's?'

'What do you say?' Dario asked Rowan. 'The Roman version of a flea market on the banks of the Tiber is something you ought to see.' Andrea, concluding her will was law, was already propelling her partner ahead.

The market was indeed a sight—even at that hour, row upon row of stalls in the glare of harsh lights, selling everything from car parts and cameras to cheap clothes and pictures, from furniture to wine and *pizzas* to be consumed on the spot.

Dr Guardia teased Andrea, 'You'd better give me your purse, in case you are tempted.' But she laughed back, 'I didn't bring any money with me. If I see anything I simply can't resist, Dario will have to finance me——' and with a hand tucked under Dario's arm, she walked away with him.

Martius Guardia looked at Rowan and smiled. 'We are put firmly in our place as stooges to the principals,' he said. Which expressed exactly her own impression of the occasion. He and she were mere sounding-boards for Andrea's self-centred vanities and for Dario's nonchalant reserves—they the experienced performers, the doctor and herself the audience, without, for her part, understanding the play.

The four met again half an hour or so later when Andrea had acquired a dented brass warming-pan, an anonymous plaster saint and a silk pennant for her car. 'All bought for me by Dario, the indulgent man!'—a claim which was at once countered by Dario's dry, 'No indulgence about it. I had no choice but to pay up if you weren't to be stopped by the stallkeeper for shoplifting as you walked away with the stuff under your arm. Do you never expect to pay cash for anything?'

She turned a seraphic smile on him. 'Never—when I have a husband or'—a calculated pause—'one of sundry old flames who'll pick up the bill for me,' she said.

Dario said, 'This one came to nineteen thousand lire. *At* your convenience, of course——'

There was no mistaking the suave repulse of

her gibe, and her sunny smile blacked out. 'Don't worry, you'll get your money,' she retorted through set teeth.

'Good,' said Dario. 'I do so dislike being typed.'

As one of your old flames—not added but to be understood, thought Rowan surprised that she should be glad Dario had had the last word.

The party broke up at the Portese Gate, Andrea telling Rowan before she drove off with Dr Guardia, 'I'll ring you, and we'll make another date.'

On their own journey back to the Villa Dario neither made nor invited any comment on the evening at all. But arrived there, as she was about to thank him and say goodnight, he surprised Rowan by asking, 'Would you care to see my father? I'm going to look in on him before I go to bed, and you can come with me if you like.'

'To see him? Yes—please.' She hesitated. 'But you said he was to have no visitors except——'

'He isn't conscious, so you can't disturb him,' Dario said shortly. 'Come along, then.'

Upstairs he led the way by a long corridor to the far end of the house, opened an outer door and knocked softly at an inner one, to be answered by the night nurse opening to him.

A hand at Rowan's back, 'My sister-in-law, Nurse Moravia,' he introduced her, his voice low. 'How is he tonight? The same?'

The nurse, a religious Sister, whispered back,

'The same. Dr Alfieri has just left. He will come again in the morning.' She stood aside, beckoning Rowan forward. 'I'm afraid he will not know you, *signora*. But come, see him——'

Rowan nodded her thanks and, followed by Dario, moved across the darkened room to the four-poster bed. The Conte lay there on his back, to her eyes the pitifully shrunken shadow of the proud figure she had glimpsed in awe in the brief moment before he had collapsed. Here, his senses arrested, he was totally vulnerable, not to be feared for any judgment he could make of her, and her compassion went out to him.

He could neither see nor hear nor expect anything of her. But *she* needed to speak to *him*, without knowing how to address him nor what to say. At last in a strangled whisper she managed, 'Father——' and laid her hand over his thin fingers clasped outside the sheet. She had surprised herself with the word, but once spoken she knew she meant to leave it there. He was Leone's father, wasn't he, and so hers by right? Dario might resent her claiming him, but the impulse to do so had come from her heart.

She stayed at his bedside while Dario talked with the nurse. Then they left. Rowan felt as grateful as she had been surprised by Dario's invitation, but on the way back to their rooms, her attempt to thank him was curtly rebuffed.

'Both nurses know you are here and might think it strange if I didn't take you to see Father,'

he said, making it clear to her hurt spirit that he
hadn't meant any generosity to her. He had only
been diplomatic, forestalling criticism before it
was voiced. She had to believe Lucia was more
genuinely kindly when the latter suggested she
might like to sit with the Conte sometimes, and
she agreed gladly. The Conte was the one person
whose blame of her hadn't been spoken—yet.

Andrea kept her promise to arrange other
meetings. She was a vivacious guide to all the
sights of Rome, and Rowan had no reason to
question her sincere disinterest until the morning
when, on their way to the prospect of the Sistine
Chapel and the Vatican Gardens, Andrea parked
in the Via Veneto, suggesting they have a coffee
first.

'I've seen the queues. They start awfully early,'
Rowan demurred.

'Yes, I know. But you have all morning, and
there's a small favour I want to ask of you. Do
you mind?' Seated at a table whose waiter seemed
bored by so early a couple of clients, Andrea went
on, 'I think we've established the habit of these
girlish outings, now, don't you?'

'I suppose so. Why?' Rowan puzzled.

'Well enough to be believed if we reported at
both ends—your end and mine—that on all of
them we spent all the time together, would you
say?'

'But we have been together every time!'

'Up to now, yes. And that's the pattern I've wanted to set. But for instance, this morning there's really no reason why you can't queue for the Vatican alone, while I go—somewhere else rather important to me, and meet you later, no one being the wiser, do you see?'

To Rowan this smelled of schoolgirl intrigue she didn't care for at all. 'No reason, I suppose,' she agreed reluctantly. 'Except that it wouldn't be true. But by "somewhere else" do you mean you're meeting some*one* else in secret?'

Andrea nodded. 'A man, of course.'

At a wild shot Rowan guessed, 'Your analyst, Doctor——?'

'*Santo cielo*, no! I don't have to meet him under a cloak. We have sessions together that Biron knows all about, and though I suspect he is in love with me, he leaves me cold. No, this is a friend who wants to know me better, and whom I've been able to see while Biron has been away. But now that he is home and I want to go out, I am never safe from being questioned. So having to keep these dates with you could be just the escape route I need. If you'll play——' Andrea appealed.

'I'm to say, if I'm asked, that we've been together all the time?'

'Only if you are asked.'

'I usually am, by either Zia Lucia or Dario.'

'Well, you don't have to elaborate. *You* will have been wherever you say you have, so you won't have to lie. We'll meet and always go back together. And it's only while Biron is at home, before he goes off somewhere else.'

'But it will mean your lying to him.'

'That's my problem.' Andrea's mouth set in an ugly line. 'All wives lie sometimes to husbands. Didn't *you*?'

'Not about anything as serious as an affair with someone else.'

'Then you were lucky,' Andrea snapped. 'Anyway, this isn't an affair yet. But it has possibilities, and I consider I deserve some.'

Lucky? Thought Rowan. Lucky—in having loved and married Leone? If only Andrea knew!

Andrea was pressing, 'So will you help—or not?' When Rowan said nothing she added craftily, 'If you won't, that's going to make worse difficulties. We'd have to stage a flaming row to explain why I wasn't playing guide to you any more, and then questions *would* be asked, believe me!'

Rowan felt trapped. She could give no possible reason for a quarrel with Andrea which either Lucia or Dario would accept without more awkward questions than she was likely to have to evade if she indulged Andrea in her nasty little plan. She said reluctantly, 'Very well. And you want to go off this morning?'

'I'll drive you to the Vactican first. And we could meet here at, say, one o'clock.'

'Where are you meeting your friend?'

'He has a studio apartment. He's an artist, a magazine illustrator, and he works from there.'

'And you're going there? Andrea, is that wise? Where is it? And what's his name?'

Andrea paid their bill and stood up. 'In case you ever have to deny anything, it might be kind of me not to tell you either,' she said, showing Rowan how thoroughly she had thought out her scheme to every detail, banking on Rowan's agreement to it, giving her little other choice. For the first time in their acquaintance, Rowan disliked Andrea heartily.

The days passed, surprising Rowan by their smooth routine. It was as if she were a genuine visitor at the Villa Cortese, instead of the virtual prisoner Dario's edict had made of her, awaiting the Conte's recovery and the inevitable disgrace which would follow.

There were times when, ashamed for the falsity of it all, she considered escape. She could manage it easily now that Andrea had shown her how to lie about her comings and goings. She had only to smuggle a few belongings out of the house and fail to meet Andrea at a rendezvous. But she wouldn't do it—couldn't. She was trusted; the Conte must be given the chance to judge her. While Dario believed her as guilty as Leone, he would not forgive her. But if time or some unknown chance should prove him wrong, he might—mightn't he? That he should; that she

would one day hear him admit her innocence
mattered to her a lot . . . too much.

And so she met Lucia and Dario at meals, sat
with the Conte in the unchanging silence of his
room, met Andrea, sometimes for genuine
errands, sometimes not; took a siesta or a swim in
the pool and once or twice was taken by Lucia to
be introduced to Cortese relatives and friends.

For Lucia, she realised, the sun rose and set
with Andrea. All her sympathy was for the
emptiness of Andrea's marriage, Andrea's childlessness, Andrea's wasted talents as a wife. On
one unguarded occasion she confided to Rowan,
'Andrea should have married Dario. He would
have appreciated her beauty and given her
children—but now it is too late. Dario will not
marry anyone else.'

So that was it—the answer to Rowan's
bewildered question of her first night. Dario had
convinced his family that, failing Andrea for his
wife, the Conte could expect no heir through
him. 'Women' for him, they might have to
accept, and Rowan felt sure they had. But it was
Andrea Bellini, on a pedestal and out of reach,
who had ordered his rejection of marriage.

The days became weeks as the specialists,
called periodically into consultation, were
guarded as to the outcome of the Conte's case. He
might recover his faculties and memory gradually.
He might regain the use of one sense, but not
another. At the most pessimistic view, his coma

could deteriorate into death; at the most optimistic but unlikely chance his recovery might be almost as sudden as his collapse—a miracle of resilience on which his family, however, mustn't rely. But perhaps . . .?

And then, by a twist of irony, it had to be Rowan, for whom his recovery held nothing but dread, who was the first witness of his return to life.

She was sitting with him as usual, relieving Lucia who had gone to siesta. As always, he lay unmoving, eyes closed, his breathing shallow. The windows of his room were wide to the hot afternoon, but a fitful shaft of sunlight was playing tricks with the dim half-light which had been prescribed for his 'rest hour'—as if it differed from any other of his comatose day.

Softly—as if she could disturb him—Rowan went to adjust the closed shutters; shut out the offending chink, and heard a whisper of sound from the bed. She turned—in time to see the long shudder of movement beneath the bedclothes, the open eyes, the sentient fingers of both hands which plucked at the hem of the covering sheet.

Scarcely daring to breathe, Rowan froze where she stood, then moved over to the bed in answer to the weak movement of the proud head. Through the bloodshot eyes, unused to normal focus for so long, Leone's father looked at her and his voice, slurred but word-perfect, said, 'I know you. You are Rowan, my son Leone's wife.'

CHAPTER FOUR

THE miracle had happened. In the private clinic to which the Conte was moved for hourly observation Dario, his only visitor, was briefed by his specialists to prompt his father's memory at first on only trivial and recent events—tests with which, as with his speech and sight and movement, the Conte had little difficulty as each day passed.

Dario reported progress. Lucia approved it. Neither of them discussed with Rowan the implications the Conte's recovery had for her; outwardly at least they were oblivious of the mental turmoil it must mean for her while she waited . . . waited for her judgment and sentence.

She found it incredible that something so vital to her could be ignored so completely in her presence. Of course it was all of a piece with their daily treatment of her and with Dario's idea of a punishing suspense for her. He *meant* her to suffer. But on the morning of the day the Conte was due home for his convalescence, her endurance gave out and she waylaid Dario to remind him.

'When your father came round the first time he had remembered me. I told you and everyone that he used my name, knew who I was. Hasn't he ever mentioned me since?'

Dario said coldly, 'Not with my encouragement.'

'Nor without it? Never questioned even why I should be there with him that afternoon? *Nothing* about me at all?' she pressed.

'Only the minimum I allowed.'

'You *allowed*!'

'I told him you took turns with us to sit with him to relieve his nurses; that you were still here as a member of the family, and when that seemed to satisfy him, I changed the subject.'

'You—changed—the—subject!' Rowan echoed again, making each word count. 'When you could have——! When, if you'd cared to, you could have—have broken the ice for both of us. Told him—Oh, but what's the use?' she broke off despairingly. 'You had only to tell him the little more that would have warned him and helped me. But you wouldn't do it, would you? He'd asked about me, and you were halfway there! But no! I must tell him myself. *I* can't change the subject. *I* must tell him that Leone lied to him; that there's no grandson for him; that I'm here under hideous false pretences—You'd risk another shock for him, but you'll have had your way with me, you sadist! And that will satisfy you, won't it? *Won't* it?' she shrilled, only to find her arms pinioned at her sides and Dario's face so close above hers that his features were out of focus.

He gave her a rough shake, let her go and straightened. 'You can cut the hysteria,' he muttered. 'It will get you nowhere. I'd been warned to keep clear of emotional issues at this stage, and I was acting to that signal when I welcomed his loss of interest in you and took him on to something else.'

'He can't have lost interest in me! He'd sent you to bring me here, and he knew I'd come. You didn't *take* him off the subject of me. You forced him!' she accused.

'Did I? Were you there?' Dario insinuated unanswerably, and she didn't try. His cool scorn of her protest was a douche to the fire of her challenge to him, and she said dully,

'When do you want me to see him?'

'After his siesta would be a good time. He probably won't get up for dinner tonight. Shall I tell him you'll go to his room at about five?' Dario asked.

'If you can bring yourself to mention my name!' was her parting barb which he ignored.

The Conte was sitting by his window and the room was full of sunshine when she obeyed his call of '*Entra*'. She thwarted his attempt to rise and took the thin hand he extended to her. Holding on to hers, he said, as he had done in that earlier darkened room, 'You are Rowan', and then, 'Sit down where I can see you, *mia figlia*. We have to talk.'

Mia figlia! He had called her 'daughter'! As

she took a chair at an angle to his she felt a glow of gratitude and was glad that at least once she had dared to call him 'father'. Shyly she agreed, 'Yes. That is why I am here, why Dario brought me to Rome, even though——'

'Even though he had to bring you alone?' the Conte prompted as she paused. 'And you were alone because you brought no child of Leone's to me; you never had one to bring?'

Surprise at the absence of anger or accusation in his tone kept her silent for a moment. Then, 'How do you know? Since when?' she urged bewilderedly. Had Dario been kinder than his threat?

He gestured vaguely. 'In my bones, for a long time, I think. For certain, in the moment when Dario brought you to me and I saw that you were alone. During my confusions I was not conscious enough to be sure. But since I have come out of them, I did not need to ask Dario if it was so; my bones' instinct had told the truth—Leone had given you no child before he died.'

'But——?' Rowan tried to work it out. 'You say you'd guessed, even before you sent Dario for me? I don't understand! You'd taken Leone's word that we had a son, and had sent money for him for *years*! Why did you do that? How could you have done it if you didn't believe it was true?'

The ghost of a smile twisted the Conte's mouth. 'Hope,' he said. 'A need to believe. You could say I gambled on a chance which my bones

knew couldn't happen—my family's first sons have
been without issue for too many generations for the
pattern to have changed in Leone. But I still
gambled—You find that difficult to credit, child?
That an old man should so crave to see his line
continue that he lets himself be fooled—hoping?'

Rowan admitted wistfully, 'It's a pride of
family, a kind of belonging I'd love to share.
Dario has it, I know.'

'As I have myself, and Dario, to a fault. It was
Leone, having none, who could devise this plot in
which you, daughter, were his willing partner or
equally his victim with us—which?'

'I certainly wasn't his partner. I knew nothing
about it,' she denied. 'But Dario refuses to
believe me, and he warned me you wouldn't
accept it either. That's why he insisted on my
coming to Rome, so that I could confess it to
your face.'

'And I too find it difficult to credit that Leone
could have kept such a secret from his wife for so
long. But I should not care to condemn you
without some proof of your guilt in it,' the Conte
allowed.

Rowan said gratefully, 'You're good. Though
why you should be more just than Dario, I don't
know.'

'Perhaps, as I was already half prepared for the
truth. I have nor needed, not been in search of an
outlet for my bitterness and disappointment as
Dario has—with reason,'

'You—with less cause than Dario to blame Leone and me? Surely not, father-in-law?'

' "Father", please, child. To address me as *suocero* is too distant. But yes, with Leone now gone beyond his blame, Dario has had to make of you a scapegoat for the betrayal of his faith in the brother who had once been his hero. Leone's defection from us four years ago was, you understand, the second treachery Dario had suffered in a couple of months. His cousin Andrea had thrown him over for Biron Bellini, and Dario's bitterness linked both as deep wrongs he could not forgive.'

'All this—before I'd even met Leone! Is Dario's blame of me fair?' Rowan protested.

'I think the wound of betrayal goes too deep to be fair.'

'But he has forgiven Andrea now. He still sees her, doesn't he?'

'Socially he has little choice. They are cousins, she is a favourite with my sister-in-law, and Andrea Bellini is a lady who does not care to see her former slaves escape,' was the Conte's shrewd comment. He went on, 'As for Leone, my anger against him, though not less than Dario's, found a different remedy. By forbidding all mention of his name in the family, I cut him out almost from memory until, with the false news of his son, I turned parent again to the extent of affording him some help with the child. My half-doubts did not creep in until after Leone's death, too late then to question him. And so I sent Dario to bring you to me, you and the child—in hope.'

'You hadn't told Dario of your doubts?' Rowan questioned.

'No one knew of them. Which made his shock the greater and his blame of you the more bitter. Has he been over-harsh with you, child?'

Harsh. Was that the right word for Dario's attempted rape of her dignity that night on the balcony? Mightn't 'pitiless' be better? Aloud Rowan said,

'Not harsh at all, whatever his feelings. He and your sister-in-law have treated me as a guest in your house while you've been ill. And now that you've been so much more fair than I deserved, I can go back to England much more happily than when I came.'

'Which cannot happen yet—your leaving us. I sent for you and Leone's son, meaning that you should both regard the Villa Cortese as your home for as long as it suited you, and that you have come alone makes no difference to the fact of your being Leone's widow, and so, deserving of our care. No,' the Conte decided for her, 'you will stay and give Dario a chance to forgive Leone through you, and you time to know and understand him for what he is—a man disappointed of a beloved woman and made callous towards all women by way of revenge—than which there are few sadder figures in nature. And so—you will stay?'

Rowan said slowly, 'I doubt if Dario will ever forgive me. Mightn't it be better if I went away?'

'But you do not want to go? You have spirit? You are challenged to show him you are not afraid to stay?'

How did he know that if she ran away it would be from Dario she would be running, defeated? He was astute and kind, and with him on her side, she could face Dario—even wanted to, which was strange ... She said, 'You make it very difficult to refuse you—Father.'

He smiled. 'And you are not refusing. That is good, and I shall see you do not regret it.' He looked at his watch. 'I think I shall go down to dinner tonight. Come back for me at eight, and I shall be seen to go down with you, on your arm. In alliance for the disarming of Dario—no?'

But before their demonstration that all was well between them there was an encounter for Rowan which she had let the Conte believe she didn't fear and which she had told herself she would almost welcome. But she still wasn't prepared for it when she saw it couldn't be escaped.

Knowing she would need only a quarter of an hour to change for the evening, she had walked out into the grounds on her way to one of her favourite haunts, the ornamental fountain spouting water from the angels' and the devils' mouths to eddy in circles in the basin below. She was sitting on the coping at her usual spot when she saw Dario and one of the gardeners talking together as they crossed the lawn towards her.

They halted and stood, finishing their discussion. The gardener went off towards the kitchen gardens and Dario came over to Rowan. Hands in trouser pockets, one foot on the coping beside her, 'You have seen my father?' he asked.

'Yes.' On a spurt of defiance she added, 'He called me daughter,' and glanced up at Dario to read the effect.

If he were surprised or impressed he gave no sign. 'Which flattered you?' he insinuated. 'Welcomed you into the family?'

'It reassured me that he wasn't judging me unheard. He said he wouldn't, without proof I was as guilty as Leone. He was just and kind, and persuaded me not to leave Rome as I had planned.'

'You agreed—when one had supposed you couldn't wait to catch the next flight out. How so?'

'That was when you had made me your prisoner until you could make me confess to your father. You assumed I shouldn't dare to defy you, and I stayed.'

'Physically I couldn't keep you. You could have walked out at any time you chose. No, it was your conscience which was your ball-and-chain, and now with my father's help you have sloughed free of that, what can possibly be keeping you here any longer?'

'I've been invited, not dragooned.'

'And perhaps are hoping for time to soften our feelings towards you?'

'If I stayed until Doomsday, would there be any prospect of that where you are concerned?' she countered.

'It might depend on your tactics. They say there is a siren in every woman which persuades her, rightly or wrongly, that she has the power to lure. But even if I should prove less than susceptible, have you any reason to fear I can't continue to treat you in a civilised way—as always?'

There was a tiny pause before she replied. Then she stood. '*Always?*' she reminded him, and turned away. Behind her she heard his short self-assured laugh, and knew he had remembered. In the next instant his hand was rough upon her arm, swinging her about to face him again. 'I agree. Body language doesn't pretend to be civilised, but now and then it can't be matched for driving its message home,' he said, and let her go.

Except that the Conte had made his promised entrance with Rowan, dinner that night followed much the same pattern as any which had gone before or were to follow it. The Conte was brought up to date with social and family news, nothing controversial was touched upon. We are four people being 'civilised', thought Rowan, and found herself wishing the Cortese code didn't discourage the public clash of temperament in which ordinary families indulged from time to time. Her own problems, the Conte's, Dario's, and for all she knew, Lucia's, were so many underground fires, damped down and smouldering, and probably the more dangerous for that.

Biron Bellini remained at home, necessitating further subterfuge on Andrea's part. Rowan visited alone the catacombs of Rome—the dim corridors of early Christian burial beneath the old Appian Way, the Borghese Gardens Zoo, the 'musts' of the Colosseum and St Peter's Dome, and Andrea had planned for her a trip to ultra-modern Rome outside the city boundaries on a morning when Dario was taking out his own car as Andrea called for Rowan who was waiting.

'Where today?' he asked.

'EUR. It's a bit of a horror, but Rowan ought to see it,' said Andrea.

Dario agreed of the Esposizione Universale di Roma, the huge area planned for Rome's world exhibition which never took place, 'Yes, it is our white elephant, the city-which-never-was, but it's worth a visit. Are you driving over?'

'Yes,' lied Andrea easily and waved a '*Ciao*' as he drove off. In fact she despatched Rowan by the underground line from Rome's railway station, arranging to keep their rendezvous at the usual time.

Rowan found EUR's great spaces, cold white buildings, dominating skyscrapers, immense sports arenas and its central artificial lake pretentious in the extreme, and as foreign from the Rome she had begun to love as would have been a settlement of igloos on its outskirts.

In the morning heat the almost empty walking areas were daunting, and after a cursory wander round she gave them best, and went back by the way she had come. In Andrea's car they would have explored further. She must remember to get Andrea to brief her on the sights she should have seen. It was becoming too easy to go along with Andrea's lies, without actually telling any . . .

It was too early to meet Andrea, so she walked through from the station to the Spanish Steps, planning to buy a posy for Lucia before crossing the south corner of Borghese to reach the top of Veneto and their usual café table.

At the foot of the Steps she was accosted by a young flower-seller who had only one bunch of rosebuds in her basket. '*Compra le rose, Signora*',' she begged Rowan who, wanting more choice, was about to move on when the girl added, 'My last flowers, *signora*—cheap. I have been here since dawn, and when I sell them I go home to care for my sick baby! *Signora*—please!'

She was pressing the bunch into Rowan's hand, and as they were fresh and a pretty pink, Rowan kept them. 'How much?' She was counting out lire from her bag when a rough voice behind her shouted, '*Lei e mentitora!*' to a background chorus of low growls.

Rowan turned to find out who was calling whom a liar, realised from the pointing and prodding fingers that it was the girl who was being accused, and that they were surrounded by a hostile crowd of flower-women and young toughs, all shouting raucous abuse.

'She lies!'

'She has no sick baby!'

'She plays the same game every day. Only one bunch left—when she has plenty. There—in the *corbello*,'—pointing to a covered basket standing in the shade.

'Here since dawn? She comes here only an hour ago, from the *trattoria* where she lives in shame with her man!'

Someone made to spit at the girl, someone else trod on her foot, and she screamed abuse back at her attackers. The crowd had spread over the roadway, obstructing the traffic; the noise from impatient car and scooter klaxons was deafening. It was the nastiest scene Rowan had ever been caught up in, but feeling she ought to defend the girl, she caught at her hand and tried to push her clear of the crowd.

But that was the signal for Rowan herself to be pushed and thumped; striving to keep her balance, she tripped over her own sandal and came down on her knees in a forest of legs and boots, threatening to trample her underfoot. Unless she used the nearest thigh as a prop she hadn't room to stand. But suddenly the forest opened up, the noise and curses subsided; Rowan glimpsed the flower-girl strolling unmolested over to her covered basket, the hooligans disappeared and neighbour was exchanging amiable talk with neighbour once more.

The police! thought Rowan. And so it was. But someone else was there. As she scrambled up, clutching handbag and mangled roses, she faced Dario, surprise and censure written all over him.

'What are you doing here?' he demanded, and as she began to explain, 'No, leave it. My car is in the queue this to-do created. Come along, I'm on my way to the office.'

She limped beside him, only too conscious of her grazed knees and palms which had taken punishment from the asphalt of the roadway, and as he showed her into the car she couldn't hide them from him.

He exclaimed over her hands and flicked aside the hem of her dress to look at her bare knees. 'Nurse must take you into the sick bay to attend to those,' he said. 'How are you placed for anti-tetanus protection?'

'I've never had to have an injection,' she told him.

'Then Nurse must give you a jab. And now, how did you come to be at the heart of that low-down squabble? I thought you and Andrea planned to go out to EUR? Why weren't you still with her, and where is she?'

Rowan had to think quickly. 'Yes—well, it was

very hot out there, and Andrea had some shopping to do.' No lie that. Andrea *always* had some shopping to do. Rowan continued, 'And after we parted, I was buying some flowers for Zia Lucia when this row flared up over the flower-girl I'd chosen, and suddenly——' she made an effort at humour which passed Dario by—'it wasn't anybody's private fight. The whole street seemed to join in. I was knocked down and couldn't claw my way out, and when I did manage to stand, it was all over.'

Dario said, 'That's the Roman temperament—fighting and calling a truce in not much more than a breath. But what about Andrea—you were to meet her to drive you home?'

Another difficulty. A glance at her watch told Rowan her rendezvous with Andrea was still an hour hence, and she could hardly convince Dario that Andrea's 'shopping' would take so long. She said evasively, 'There was nothing definite. Actually I meant to walk back to the Villa across the Gardens. But now——'

'Now I shall drive you home when Sister Bezzio, our industrial nurse, has finished with you,' said Dario as the uniformed usher to the Cortese Estates building sprang to open the car door.

Rowan had never been inside the offices before. There was an immense foyer and a magnificent curving staircase of black marble leading to a mezzanine floor above, the staircase being probably a showpiece, secondary in use to the long bank of elevators, one of which was opened in readiness by a page when Dario approached it.

His office on the fifth floor was furnished in gleaming mahogany and green leather. Wall mirrors gave an illusion of even greater size to the big room, and from the chair to which Dario invited her, Rowan faced a discouraging reflection of her smudged face, wild hair and soiled dress.

Dario flicked a telephone switch on his desk, spoke, and when there was a knock at the door, went to open it to a nurse whom he introduced to Rowan, explaining, 'My sister-in-law has been unfortunate enough to tangle in a street brawl. Do you necessary for her, will you, Sister, and start her on a course of anti-tetanus serum, please.'

Sister Bezzio clucked in concern over Rowan's injuries and took her away to the clinic adjoining the personnel office on the top floor. Rowan's hands and knees were bathed and strapped; she was furnished with a record card and told she must have a boost to her injection in six weeks' time. Sister Bezzio helped her to freshen up and to sponge her dress; she drank a cup of strong black coffee and was duly returned to Dario's office in better order than when she had left it.

His secretary was with him, taking dictation. He signalled to Rowan his need to finish, then he was ready to drive her back to the villa.

All this had taken some time; Andrea would already have gone to Veneto, waited no doubt, then given her up. If Andrea had then driven back to the villa, how they were going to synchronise their stories of their failure to meet was a problem Rowan hadn't solved before she and Dario arrived themselves.

Andrea's car was on the drive. Andrea was in the *salotto* with Lucia. Rowan looked an appeal to Andrea to leave the explanations to her, but Andrea burst out, 'So *there* you are! Why didn't you wait for me? I wasn't late——' She broke off at seeing Dario behind Rowan. 'Oh, I see—you collected Dario instead, and abandoned me!' Then, noticing Rowan's bandaged hands, '*Santo cielo!* How did that happen? Your legs too—you have had a fall?'

Rowan explained to a murmur of sympathetic noises from Lucia. She finished, 'I was lucky that Dario was passing in his car. He has had me treated by his nurse at the offices, and now I'm fine.'

Andrea said suspiciously, 'All this in the few minutes before our date? You must have been super-punctual; I drove by that way on my way to Veneto, and there wasn't a sign of there having been a scrap.'

'Oh well—yes. That is, I didn't realise we'd made a date,' Rowan floundered. 'I thought, *when you went shopping*, I said I would walk back across the Gardens—don't you remember?'

She was relieved that she seemed to have made her point when Andrea slapped her temple, exclaiming, 'But of course—stupid me! When I left you, just to pop into Gucci's for something for Biron, we weren't going to meet again, were we? Anyway, I'm glad you are none the worse for my leaving you on your own for a few minutes.' She switched her attention to Dario. 'A message for you from Biron, my friend. He is off again tomorrow to the Italian bloodstock sales, and as he hasn't met Rowan yet, he suggests we make a party, the four of us, for *Aida* at the Caracalla Baths tonight. Will you bring Rowan along?'

Dario looked at Rowan. 'I hardly think— Another night might be better. Rowan has had pain-killers and an anti-tetanus jab.'

'But I've told you—it is Biron's last night, and Rowan says she is fine now,' Andrea broke in impatiently. 'Besides, he has tickets.'

Suspecting Dario might have his own reasons for appearing to consider her, Rowan said, 'I'm all right now. I could go,' and Lucia murmured, 'One should never see *Aida* anywhere other than at Caracalla. The spectacle and the sound are unforgettable. If Rowan feels equal to it, Dario, why not?'

Andrea took Dario's slight nod as his consent. 'You will dine with us first, and then we'll go on,' she said, adding to Rowan, 'Have a good siesta this afternoon, *cara. Aida* is long, and we shall be late.'

The Bellinis' villa on the New Appian Way was a white ultra-modern building with the mansions of famous film stars for its neighbours. From the number of staff it employed it seemed to Rowan that Andrea had some reason for boredom, if not for infidelity. There was practically nothing Andrea *had* to do at any hour of the day. (Though am I any less idle than she is while I linger on here? was Rowan's following guilty thought.) Nothing could be more purposeless than the life she was leading. And yet it was not only the Conte's persuasion of her which kept her in Rome. There was another pull against her will to leave. She had no faith in the improbable hope that in time Dario would soften towards her, but there was a charisma about him which she found almost hypnotic in its power. It drew her into conflict with his hostility, beating vainly, she knew, but wanting from him the same justice as she had from his father, wanting it . . . too much.

Biron Bellini was a florid self-important character. He wore too many ostentatious rings on fat fingers, and his conversation was mostly limited to horse-breeding affairs. But he seemed very conscious of where one should be 'seen' or not 'seen' in Roman society.

'Of course *Aida* at Caracalla is a shockingly tourist thing to do,' his snobbery informed Rowan. 'Ten thousand in the amphitheatre audience in the open air every night. Very plebeian; one needn't even *dress*, though you girls like to. But when the Opera House closes for the summer, Caracalla comes into its own. And one can't deny the masses do enjoy going berserk over all those elephants and horse-drawn chariots on stage.'

'Well, I'm sure I'm tourist enough to enjoy it,' said Rowan.

'You—tourist? Surely not?' he scoffed. 'One supposed you to be making your home at the Villa Cortese, recovering from your loss, and perhaps until you marry again—if you want to. Meanwhile, I have to thank you for being such a charming companion for Andrea—making her loneliness tolerable when I have to be away.'

And making it possible for her to lie to you when you're at home—was a thought Rowan naturally did not voice.

The performance of *Aida* against the background of the centuries old Roman remains was all Rowan could have hoped of its colour and music and drama on the vast stage in windless night warmth and under a canopy of stars. The only jarring effect was the intermittent flash of cameras—forbidden, but the rule ignored. But when she thought of the hundreds of homes, from Chicago to Tokyo, from Melbourne to Oslo, where the pictures would be shown, she blinked every time and forgave the users. In a kind of 'high' of pleasure, she would have forgiven anyone anything tonight, even Dario, conscious in a new way of his nearness beside her, of the causal brush of his sleeve against her bare arm, of his lifted profile glimpsed against the dark sky.

Between the acts of the opera, they walked in the grounds and visited the bar, where Dario, hearing Biron order for Rowan, interposed curtly, 'No drink for Rowan. She has had sedatives, and they don't mix.'

Biron protested, 'Oh, nonsense! If not spirits, a glass of our innocent white *Albana* has no more potency than sherbet. It can't hurt her.'

Dario shrugged and spoke directly to Rowan. 'You won't take any alcohol tonight. That's an order,' he said, and knowing he was right, she obeyed him. Biron scoffed, 'The man has you under his thumb. You couldn't be more submissive if you were married to him! I declare, *I* dare not police Andrea so!'

It was towards the end of the third act that Rowan became aware of the increasing ache in her legs and hands. The pain-killing effects were wearing off, she supposed. Then her temples and her upper lip were damp and there was a prickle of gooseflesh all over her body, in spite of the warmth of the night. That must be a reaction of fever to the serum, and at the end of the act, when the others left for the interval, she elected to stay where she was, praying she could last the evening out without making a fool of herself.

She was lightheadedly aware of the returning audience and of the rise of the curtain for the final scenes. But the music reached her ears in

waves of magnified and receding sound, and at
the first camera flash she started with shock and
felt, rather than saw, Dario turn to scan the
drained pallor of her face.

In a hoarse whisper he questioned, 'What——?'
and put an arm round her shoulders. Her eyes
weren't focussing properly and she leaned against
him, thankful to close them against his shoulder.
She heard the stir among their neighbours as he
helped her into the nearest aisle. Then they were
free of the auditorium and he was asking her if
she could walk to the car.

She answered stupidly, 'Must we miss the last
act?'

'Of course. You are ill. I am taking you home,'
he said.

For almost the first time the Villa Cortese,
offering a bed and perhaps peace from this
drumming in her ears, sounded like home. Dario
repeated his question and she nodded, 'I can
walk, if you'll go slowly,' and added as a further
experiment with speech, 'I'm not really ill. Just—
not—very well.'

In the car she must have dozed, for the next
thing she knew plainly was that they were in the
hall of the house, where Dario, without consulting
her this time, lifted her with consummate ease
and carried her upstairs. He kept a welcome arm
round her while he opened her door and helped
her to a chair. 'I'll call Maria to you,' he said.

'Oh no, please, don't get her up,' Rowan

begged. 'I only want to get undressed and into bed.'

'Where do you keep your robe?' was his answer to that, as he handed her her nightgown from the turned-down bed.

'In the shower-room, hanging on the door.'

He went with her there. 'I'll wait,' he said, and turned back into the bedroom.

She undressed dazedly, almost pitching forward when she stepped out of her clothes and tried to pick them up from the floor. When she went back, Dario must have fetched a clinical thermometer, for he had it ready to slip under her tongue when he had helped her into bed. He shook it down without telling her what its reading had been, and covered her over when she lay back on her pillow. 'You won't get up in the morning until the doctor has seen you,' he ordered, and she acquiesced with a nod. Oddly, so desperate was her need for sleep that she felt no embarrassment with him. He was a ministering nurse, with a nurse's right to order her to undress and be put to bed and to do as she was told.

He wasn't Dario, he wasn't Leone, the only other man to have glimpsed her near-nudity in a filmy nightgown. If he could only stay as impassive and uncritical as this—— But what thought she had meant to follow her 'If only' was lost in the cloud of sleep which took over her senses. She saw his hand linger to smooth the turned-back sheet, knew that he had moved towards the door and had clicked off the light. After that—nothing.

It was still dark when she woke again from a dream sleep which had followed that drugged torpor.

She lay on her back, recalling the dream in all its upset of reason, its absurdity. She had been here in bed, as she was still, and Dario—*Dario*! had come over to the bedside, touched her hair, smiled down at her and stooped to kiss her on the lips, just as Leone, surprising her from sleep, might have done, teasing her with a 'darling lazybones,' or some such quip.

But the man who had kissed her in her dream had called her distinctly, 'my darling liar'—and he hadn't been Leone. He had been Dario.

Her eyes growing used to the dark, she turned on her side to look across towards the window. In a chair there, seemingly asleep with his cheek resting on his palm, eyes closed, was Dario, the real Dario.

When he had put out the light she thought he had gone out of the room after doing it. But instead he must have stayed with her. Propped on her elbow, she lay watching him, puzzled by a concern which had kept him there, in case she woke or needed anything. It was all of a piece with his brusque care of her last night—playing fair when his enemy was down. It seemed he was half human after all . . .

CHAPTER FIVE

WHEN she had waked again it had been full daylight, and of course Dario had gone.

During the morning the doctor came to confirm that hers was the one system in thousands which reacted violently to certain vaccines. All the better, he had assured her cheerily. It showed the serum had done its work.

Lucia had come to muse aloud, 'When we were young and had a fall, we washed the place with disinfectant and were none the worse; now, it seems, it has to be drugs, drugs with everything'—putting modern medicine where she considered it belonged.

The Conte had come, commiserating that it was too bad that Rowan had missed the last act of *Aida*. It was the most poignant, with the lovers faithful even into the tomb. Dario must take her to see it again some day. There was plenty of time——

Andrea, busy getting Biron off to Milan, had not come but had telephoned, clucking sympathy and commenting, 'That was a narrow escape we had yesterday noon. But you handled it beautifully, and now you can have a clear conscience. While Biron is away I can manage my innocent little intrigue without involving you. My love to Dario. *Ciao.*'

During the day Dario had not come, and when at dinner that night he did not mention having spent the night in her room, Rowan did not tell him she knew he had. She had an idea he would not care to have been surprised, vulnerable in sleep in a way which, awake, he never was. Drowsily, last night, before she had slept again, she had wondered how often Andrea might have seen him so, spent and relaxed with love, before she had jilted him for Biron Bellini, turning him into the steely intolerant he was today. It had been a distasteful picture which sleep had had to blot out. Yet here it was again today, part of a growing curiosity about Dario the man, fed by his father's eager talk of his remaining son.

The Conte sought her company often, encouraging her Italian and practising his own English. He filled in history for her by describing the Rome of his boyhood and the faction-torn Italy of his grandparents. He was '*il Conte Cortese*', he told her, only by his family's outworn claim to a nobility which the Republic of the present day did not recognise.

'Had Leone lived, the title would have gone to him after my death. But Dario does not want it, saying that to be a *signor* of Rome is good enough for any man. Though if any *woman* will content herself with plain 'Signora' if 'Contessa' is within her reach remains to be seen when he takes a

wife. As of course he will. He knows his duty to
our line—that it must go on,' the Conte
concluded with typical Cortese arrogance, Rowan
considered.

It was such cues which found her a captive
listener in her questing need to learn more of the
man whose challenge was never far from her
mind. Since that first fevered dream of Dario, his
image had intruded more than once again—
enigmatic, mocking, and when she was awake
there was always this driving compulsion to hear
his name spoken, to use it herself.

She remembered a similar need to talk of
Leone to other people. But she had loved Leone,
so there could be no comparison with this
needling interest in Dario, could there? And yet
Dario as a boy, as Andrea's suitor, as the shrewd
director of Cortese Estates, as woman-despiser,
became the more sharply defined as her memory
of Leone, husband and lover and . . . liar faded.
Dario was now her present. Leone was fast
becoming her past.

One afternoon she was reading on the balcony
to her room when Dario came across from his
own balcony to draw up a chair beside her. She
used a finger as a bookmark, but found the book
taken from her and closed. As she looked her
question without speaking he answered it.

'I have a message for you from my father,' he
said. 'How long have you been here with us
now?'

She calculated. 'Three, nearly four months.'

He agreed, quoting, 'First "dragooned" and then "invited",' and watched her flush. 'And in that time you'll have realised that Father has grown fond of you?'

'He has let me hope so,' she admitted, pleased.

'And is now so willingly aware of your rights as Leone's widow that he proposes to settle on you half the assets of Cortese Estates——' At Rowan's start of aghast protest Dario lifted a silencing hand. 'Not as a bequest to you on his death, but now, as soon as it can be arranged. He sees it as his duty to you and wants to show how much of his favour you have gained in a very short time.'

Rowan could only stare, open-mouthed. At last she managed, 'But this is absurd! I have no rights through Leone. Your father had cut him off. I expect nothing from your family. I never have——!'

'Even to the stiffnecked gesture of leaving your sponsored bank account untouched?' Dario insinuated.

'Yes, even to that,' she bit out. And then, 'How did you know?'

'One has sources,' he shrugged. His glance, mock-appreciative, travelled over her shining hair to bare shoulders and the revealing line of the short white shift, waisted with a gold cord. 'I must say you manage very well on what must be a shoestring budget,' he added.

'Thank you,' she sneered, and as a thought struck her, 'You mentioned my "favour" with the Conte. Do you suspect me of having worked for this utterly unacceptable idea of money for me?'

Dario's eyes absently followed the vapour trail of a passing aircraft. 'The uncharitable could have doubts, I admit,' he murmured. 'The biddable proxy daughter, all gentle compliance, all switched-on charm——'

At that her open palm lunged to hit him, but her wrist was instantly caught in his grip and shaken before it was flung back at her. She panted at him, 'You're so bitter, it simply passes belief! How dare you imply your father would fall for wiles like that? He likes me, he's forgiven me. He's good and kind——'

'Needing no persuasion at all that he owes this duty to you?'

'Certainly none from me. And half the Cortese assets! As if I could manage money on that scale!'

Dario commented, 'If you had it, I daresay the money boffins would fall over themselves to advise you, and the columnists could go to town on the subject of Tragic Widow Heiress. But I admit the arrangement would give you such power as the firm can ill afford to vest in one person, making the proposal an eccentricity of my father's which I have had to persuade him is impossible for Cortese to entertain.'

'Then why bother to bring such an outrageous suggestion to me?' Rowan parried.

'Because, as a condition of his conceding that the firm couldn't wear it, Father insisted that you know he made it before I put to you my alternative plan which could serve his purpose of care for your future equally well. May I outline it to you?'

'There's no *need* for any alternative!'

'As your next of kin through Leone, we consider there is. As one of our family, you are our responsibility, and your marriage to me which I am proposing to you now seems the best way of discharging it. What have you to say?'

At the fatal word 'marriage' Rowan's hands had clasped to knuckle-whiteness in her lap. Her snap reaction was that she must be dreaming again. Dario could *not* have said what she thought she had heard, proposing he should marry her, the chosen enemy he loved to hate! Such an absurdity could only occur in a dream—— And yet the reality of the hot, bright afternoon was all around her; Dario, darkly vital as always, was no phantom of the night, but there in the flesh, watching her for her response to the monstrous suggestion he had seriously made.

He had meant it. The Conte had agreed to it, betraying her. She controlled her sense of outrage to say at last, 'If I called you mad, that would be charitable of me. For how in your right senses you could believe I could consider anything so unthinkable I can't imagine. Marriage to me, when you hate and despise me as you do, and as your father can't help but know?'

'Does he?' Dario drawled.

She flinched. 'Meaning that only you know the depth of your contempt? Yes, I can believe that. So how could you think of marrying me for any reason in the world? In common justice to yourself at least, if not in even ordinary humanity to me?'

Dario said coldly, 'I'd have thought the humanity aspect could be covered by the rights and privileges, not to mention a life interest share in my wealth, which your becoming my wife would afford you.'

'Security and rights at a price I'm not prepared to pay!' she defied.

'Though isn't there another aspect which perhaps you ought to consider?' Dario countered suavely. 'Remember that you have a debt to my father, to the family, which you can only hope to repay by giving him the grandchild you and Leone chose to pretend you had. I know Nature saw to it that you hadn't one to bring him, but at least you could have spared him the vain hope that you had. Which brings us back to my offer of marriage which, if you accept it, will at least afford you the promise of atonement for wrongs done. In short, and bluntly—a child or children by me should set your obligation record straight.' As he saw Rowan was about to speak his raised hand stopped her again.

'As for your concern about justice to me,' he went on, 'I hope you won't lose any sleep over

that. The Cortese family's future is as important
to me as it is to Father, and being uncommitted
elsewhere, I'm quite willing to entertain a
marriage which will content him for you, and
afford me the role which, with a bride of your
admitted attraction, a good many men might
envy me, I think.'

'The role of an unloved husband to a hated
wife? You would settle for that, for the gamble of
fathering children who might not happen?'
Rowan scorned, despising herself for sinking to
plead sanity with him.

'Barrenness is a risk any marriage takes,' he
pointed out.

'And so?'

'And so, in a business marriage such as this,
one needn't be blinded by romance but can
choose for the quality of the womanflesh which is
likely to produce results.'

Rowan's senses churned with horror at the
deliberate crudity. But she would *not* appeal to
his compassion. On his own level of raw
detachment she said, 'Patting a particular heifer
on the flank and telling the cattle vendor, "I'll
take this one for breeding"?'

He evinced no shame. 'Something like that,' he
allowed.

'Promising the womanflesh her keep for life on
condition she produces results?'

'More than her bare keep; standing and
acceptance. But going along with the luck of the

draw, whether or not she produced results—in which event, too bad for the plan. A Cortese marriage is a permanence from which she shouldn't expect release.'

'And supposing——' Rowan held his glance with all the meaning she could bring to her own—'supposing she wilfully withheld results, what then?'

Dario shrugged. 'A bridge to be crossed if ever reached.' But behind the nonchalance she read danger and decided against pressing him for an answer.

She stood up. 'I've heard enough,' she said. 'You and the Conte hatched your plan and he sent you to me with it——'

'Even he "sends" me nowhere,' Dario remarked.

She brushed the quibble aside. 'You brought it and you can take it back again. But not before I've seen the Conte myself. When shall I go to him?'

'He is waiting for you, expecting you.'

'Thank you.' At the open french window to her room she paused. 'Womanflesh' had to be avenged ... 'I believe there's a name for a man like you. Rather a coarse one—*stud*. Does it fit?' she asked.

Though Dario made no movement, gave no sign, she might have been warned by a red snap of anger deep in his eyes. But she was not. She had turned away too soon.

An hour later she was back in her room, her interview with the Conte behind her and hours of self-chosen solitude before her. When she had parted from him she had asked that until she left the Villa the next morning she need not meet anyone but the domestic staff who would see her off.

'If I may, I'd like to have dinner in my room,' she said. 'And I'd be grateful if you would explain and apologise for my leaving to your sister-in-law; thanking her too for all she has done for me.' To which the Conte had agreed with a morose disappointment which she could not bring herself to pity. She had been touched by the quiet dignity of his, 'So be it, if that's the way you want it, daughter, though I can only say I am very, very sorry.' But he had abetted Dario in his infamous scheme, welcomed it, hadn't he? She couldn't afford to be charitable.

Though her pride needed to make her own arrangements for her departure, he had insisted that Dario must handle them for her. Dario would book her seat on the early morning London flight; she would be driven to the airport in time to catch it, and the Conte hoped she would use the international telephone to make any appointments to be met at the other end.

But there was no one who could meet her at such short notice. She would have to make her own way back to the flat she had left four months ago at Dario's command. Meanwhile her packing was little more than the flinging of necessities into a couple of cases. She had all the evening and the long night for thought and anger to curdle. For the first and only time she had bested Dario, had said No to him, and by leaving was showing both him and the Conte that she meant it.

But final and definite as her victory was, it was a sour triumph. Dario had given no sign of having accepted defeat. She supposed he would remember her only as a failed project in his career. He would have to make another soulless choice of woman for begetting his children; the Conte had made no secret of his displeasure at her rejection of his generosity. He would write her off as an ingrate; Dario had never regarded her as anything but a nothing-worth. She would leave no kindly thought of her behind at the Villa Cortese, where she remembered once to have thought she would love to belong.

The evening darkened about her. A maid came with an envelope containing her seat reservation and baggage insurance for her flight. An hour later the same girl brought a dinner tray of melon, sliced veal in a sweet-sour sauce, a bottle of white wine and fresh peaches. Rowan had little appetite for it, and though her isolation was of her own choosing, she felt like a child who had been banished for bad behaviour. The very silence of the house seemed to dismiss her. The Villa Cortese and

Leone's family had finished with her. She would not see any of them again.

She had a bath and prepared for bed. No need to set the alarm of her travelling clock; she knew she would be nervously awake in the morning. It was soon after she had heard a city clock chime eleven that there was a knock at her door, just one, followed by silence when she did not answer at once.

She waited, and then, on some premonition that this was no maid with a belated message, she slipped from bed and went to open the door.

It was Dario who stood there. What sixth sense had told her it would be? And what reckless impulse had tempted her to open to him? She must be mad!

She backed away from him. 'What do you want?'

He didn't answer. He thrust to the door behind him and followed her retreat. She turned her back on him and his hand went to her shoulder, swinging her about and so close to him that his breath fanned her, an animal heat.

Frightened, she accused, 'You're——!'

'—Not drunk,' he finished for her, his diction clear and incisive. 'Simply calling socially for the purpose of proving "stud" to a lady's satisfaction and as a parting gift——'

His arms went about her, moulding her to the hard contours of his body, holding back his head so that he could watch the panic in her eyes.

Rowan dared not scream. The choking protest that reached her lips was bruised into silence by the brutish pressure of a mouth intent on punishment, on revenge. Now he was forcing her back towards the bed where, when she stumbled over the hem of her nightgown, he caught up its fullness and swathed her in it, mummy-like, before thrusting her flat upon the bed.

Her arms flailed, her hands clawed at him, but the gown swaddled the lower half of her body and legs, and his seated bulk, pressed close to her side, barred her escape. She wished she knew the kind of language a man, so cornered, would use. As it was, dumb in physical defeat, she had to wait his pleasure in releasing her.

He eased his own position, crossing a leg and arching an arm to press down on the bed at her far side. For a tense beat of time he stared at her; she at him. Then he said thickly, 'Well, my pretty tramp, you asked for this, didn't you? Deliberately, perhaps? Expecting it? Even wanting it—not so?'

'Wanting it? Wanting you? No!'

'Naming me for a stud, but not wanting evidence of my bestiality in order to prove yourself right?' Dario shook his head. 'I'm afraid I can't believe you, sister-in-law. You wouldn't have chosen the word with such venom if you hadn't meant it to provoke. So here's a sample of the action, my dear—with the breeder's compliments——'

With an agile twist of his body he was full length beside her, thighs aligned to hers, his hands travelling, touching, exploring. One of them in a pseudo-caress tightened momentarily and cruelly on her throat. The narrow straps of her nightgown were slid from her shoulders, the swell of her breasts exposed, the line of her diaphragm traced by both his hands to her waist. There they hovered, as if he were savouring the threat of allowing them further past the jut of hip and soft roundness of thigh to reserves which she must keep from him at all costs. Dear God, he couldn't mean to take her by force—could he?

His hands came up again to cup her face; his assault on her mouth was slow, deliberate, even gently teasing at first, a featherlight touch that invited, then deepened and hardened and demanded and became a hot fire of desire which, to her shame, was tinder to her senses, hungry for stimulation for too long. Her turning and twisting against the iron of his hold went slack as an ebbing tide and she was clinging wildly, her fingers scrabbling at the flesh beneath his thin evening shirt, drawing him to her, moving against him in abject invitation to a body which was using her not even for its own pleasure but for hate.

Conscious thought hazed into pure sensation; she was all flesh and quivering nerves, and past any will to repulse him, when suddenly his rejection of her was as violently total as his assault had been brutal. He put her from him and stood up, stood over her, his scrutiny of her as clinical and detached as if he had had nothing to do with her subjection. He said, 'Perhaps it would be a pity to take the lesson to its climax. Judging by present showing, you might enjoy it too much, and that would be to defeat the object of the exercise.'

As she struggled to pull herself upright, he flicked a fingernail against her cheek. 'Goodnight and goodbye, sister-in-law,' he told her. 'You chose the wrong brother to marry, and the wrong one to try to fool. Hard luck. Next time, if you put that undoubted libido of yours to good use, you might get yourself a *man!*'

When he had gone Rowan could not even cry. She could only bury her head in a pillow, an ostrich in sand, a worm scurrying for earth cover—for shame and humiliation and the ache of a frustration which was the most painful and shaming of all.

She had yielded to Dario's body, wanted it, remembered his touch with ecstasy still. While he had flayed her with his scorn she had glowed for him, her whole body a blush of desire. His pretence of passion had made her his creature, his slave, and had left her with neither dignity nor pride while he used it on her.

She had been as mindlessly animal as he. Nothing to choose between them then. Nothing more to be said. Only for her now the vain hauntings of some might-have-beens. If Leone hadn't been a cheat. If Dario hadn't hated her at their very first meeting. If the Conte hadn't let her think he cared as much for her happiness as for his Cortese line. If Dario had ever softened his attitude, tolerated her, liked her, ever—kissed her because he wanted to—These were the things which hadn't happened and wouldn't, and she had to learn to live with knowing that.

London offered a cold August day for her welcome back. She had heard an outward Rome flight being finally called, and on the long walk to the luggage and passport check-out she envied the people hurrying eagerly the other way. She was coming back to a closed-up apartment, no job and a crowd of bitter memories. She owed the Conte and Lucia the courtesy of an 'Arrived Safely' message, but she expected no reply and received none.

The need of a job was a priority and her main headache. The school secretarial posts would all be filled for the coming term and she did not succeed anywhere by the time term had begun. That meant little chance until January, and her budget would be badly strained by then. She thought of the bank account which had been opened for her in Rome, and got some wry satisfaction from thinking of its being closed without a single cheque having been drawn on it.

In between doing some freelance copy typing

she went about the tasks of house-hunting for a
small and cheaper apartment, and of tidying and
clearing her present one in preparation for a
move. She decided she must be ruthless with
mementoes of her life with Leone which she had
kept for sentiment's sake. Silly legends had been
woven round such inanimates as a bent silver
butter knife and an outworn clothes-brush, but
the memories they evoked had been soured for
her now and they must go. But it was with
reluctance that she came at last to the discarding
of a long-untouched sweater and cap of Leone's
flung carelessly by him into the dark back of a
wardrobe and left there by herself after his death.
She had known they were there, but while they
were wearable they had been favourite gear of
his, and so, part of what he had been.

She steeled herself to reach for them, shook out
the badly creased sweater, darned elbows and all.
There was a small bulge in a pocket, an envelope
sealed and folded once on the message in Leone's
writing, 'Rowan, the Bank will have this for you
if I should go suddenly'—and signed with his
name. Inside the envelope there was another, also
sealed, and this, heart thumping with apprehen-
sion, she tore open to read on the single sheet of
paper within,

'If I have tried and failed to knock down a bus,
or been felled by any other means, this you must
know about me now, if you haven't learned it
already.

'I have cheated on the family and on you, Rowan *cara*. I have claimed we have a son, even named him Scipio Cortese, and have taken regular large remittances from Father for his keep over—yes, more than two years. I don't know how I mean the bluff to end. The money has been too welcome, so that if the story is still running when I go, I must leave the mess to you.

'Forgive me if you can. This—to prove to anyone concerned—that I have acted alone and you know nothing about it.

'Please God you never have to read this. *Ciao*. Leone.'

Weak-legged and trembling, Rowan huddled on the floor where she had knelt to retrieve the sweater. She read and re-read the letter until the words danced before her eyes. Neither covering envelope nor letter was dated and she had to guess at the history of the package which had never reached the Bank as Leone had intended it should. Therefore, since he couldn't possibly have meant to abandon it carelessly in a pocket, the letter must have been written only very shortly before his fatal accident. He hadn't given himself time to take it to the Bank. Which meant—only slowly did her reeling brain take in the truth—that she had here Leone's signed proof of her innocence of his plot, until he had died, taking his secret with him.

To anyone concerned—he had written. That meant Dario. Here in her hand was the evidence she could have thrown in his handsome face. But it was too late now. She had cut herself adrift from the Corteses. And even if she had not—the rash defiance of the decision took her by surprise—*she would not have produced it to him*. Let him believe her on her own given word or not at all. If they ever met again the very possession of Leone's letter would lend her a secret power which would taste the sweeter for being withheld . . .

An afternoon or two later she returned from an abortive apartment search to hear at the manager's office that she had had a male visitor who had left a message saying he would call back later—at six.

'He didn't leave his name?' Rowan envisaged a possible friend of Leone's.

'No, but I think I recognised him,' the chatty girl clerk volunteered. 'I'm pretty sure he was the Italian man—your brother-in-law, didn't you say he was?—who took you to Italy with him in the spring. So awfully like your husband, Mrs Cortese, I thought——'

Dario—in London to see her again? Impossible. 'I shouldn't think so. Signor Cortese wouldn't just arrive. He would have let me know,' she told the girl, who shrugged, 'Oh well, I was wrong.'

She was not wrong, and Rowan's instinct knew it. No one could outwardly resemble Leone as Dario did, and when Rowan opened her door at six o'clock, she knew it would be Dario standing there, history repeating itself—for what purpose this time?

He came in and made his greeting a question. 'You were told to expect me?'

'To expect a caller. You didn't leave your name at the desk.'

'In case you refused to see me, which would have been your privilege.'

'It would, wouldn't it?' she agreed. 'And could you have been surprised if I had used it?'

'After our parting in Rome? Yes, perhaps I guessed you would and I didn't care to risk it.' He looked about him. 'Won't you sit down? And may I?'

As she sat, 'And if I had refused, what then?'

'I'd have had to resort to tiresome methods— following you in the street, accosting you. A nuisance for me and an annoyance for you, but necessary, since I am not going back to Rome without telling you what I came to say and insisting that you listen.'

'Only listen?'

'And act, if you agree with me that you should. You will have heard nothing from us, so you won't know that Father's health has deteriorated since you left. He has lost spirit and verve, and though his symptoms are physical, both he and I know the trouble is that he is missing you badly. He was stunned by your rejection of his plan to keep you in the family, and ever since has been torturing himsef as to where he went wrong.'

Rowan said coldly, 'I'm surprised you can believe he could possibly miss a gold-digging proxy daughter like me. And I thought I'd made it quite clear to you both that I wasn't to be bought at any price to be a—a——'

'"A milch cow to the Cortese clan" is probably the phrase you want, isn't it?' Dario supplied. 'Yes, well—this he accepted in the shock of the moment, but he hasn't since been able to credit that you meant it. And in view of the danger that he may slip back physically even further, I am putting to you that it could be your duty to come back to Rome to make your peace with him before it is too late.'

'After your parting from me, and on those conditions—never!' Rowan shuddered.

'You can afford to forgive him without having to forgive me,' Dario pointed out.

'I can forgive him from here.'

'With nothing of the convincing effect your voluntary return with me would have. But you must let your conscience decide.' He rose and put aside his chair. 'You have work which would delay your coming at once?'

She could have told him Yes, firmly scotching the notion that she could leave within hours. But she hesitated and was lost.

'Yes, no—that is, I'm only working freelance at the moment,' she admitted.

'Then you could come within a matter of days?'

'If I decided to come.'

'And would stay, without considering yourself "bought" or in danger of being dragged to the altar?'

'If I came for anything longer than a short visit as the Conte's guest, I should hope to find some work. I'm bi-lingual, and there must be some openings for secretaries in the city.'

Dario said curtly, 'Cortese women of your standing do not "work". However——' He took a card from his wallet. 'My hotel—the same as last time. I shall expect you to call me with your decision.'

'And if it's No?'

'In that case, you needn't bother to ring, for we shall have nothing more to say to each other,' he chilled her with brusque finality on his way to the door.

In spite of her defiant front, he left her disturbed and uncertain. Skilled as always, he had made his appeal to her conscience the thread with which to twitch her back to Rome on this errand of charity to his father. And—she *wanted* to go back. She actively missed the challenge she had met in the Villa Cortese. Yes, incredibly she was homesick for Rome. On the other hand, she mustn't run to it as a refuge from loneliness and lack of work here in London.

That weighed with her until it occurred to her that in going back merely for an open-ended visit to make her peace with the Conte, she was committing herself to nothing, had nothing to lose. Nothing but a rag of pride if she said Yes to Dario.

She gave him time and more to get back to his hotel. Then she rang the number and asked to have him paged.

CHAPTER SIX

Rowan's reception on her return with Dario had been typical of the Cortese family's reserves. Outwardly she might never have left the Villa in the circumstances she had when the Conte had kissed her warmly in greeting, and neither he nor Lucia had embarrassed her with a word of reproach.

Afternoon tea in delicate porcelain had been dispensed by Lucia in the sun-suffused *salotto*, and the talk had been of the news Rowan had missed while she had been in England.

Biron Bellini was away from home on another trip. Cousin Cecilia Salvati of Verona had had her baby, a fine boy. There were some enchanting new lion cubs in the Borghese Gardens Zoo. The Opera House promised an outstanding winter season, and 'everyone' would be at the opening night. *Aida*, it so happened. Dario must partner Rowan to it. A party for it must be arranged . . .

It had been so conventional a welcome from hosts to guest that Rowan had distrusted it, seeing Dario's diplomatic hand behind it. She envisaged his briefing to the Conte, 'Let her down lightly, and she'll come round', or something equally cynical. For she thought neither the Conte nor Lucia could possibly forgive so lightly her rejection of them and Dario. At his direction they were acting a part, and she must expect inevitable bitterness to break surface later, making her position intolerable unless she made her motives clear from the outset. Namely, that she had come back out of concern for the Conte, not as a cringing prodigal, nor a turncoat on her pride. She would stay as the Villa's guest for as long as it appeared to want her. *But* not accepting its charity for any longer than it took her to achieve some independence with a job.

Knowing she would get no help from Dario, she went straight to his father, explaining as tactfully as she could that though she was grateful for his hospitality, she was a working girl by habit, not used to the idleness a stay of more than a few weeks would ask of her. She found the Conte less prejudiced than Dario had sounded, but vague as to ways and means.

'You would like to be occupied as a secretary. But wouldn't your being English put you at a disadvantage for an Italian post?' he demurred.

'For a good many, yes,' Rowan allowed. 'But I'm bi-lingual, and I'd thought that in, say, a travel agency or a hotel or an export office I might be of use.'

'If you succeeded, you would keep office hours. We should not see as much of you as we should like,' he objected.

She threw him a grateful smile. 'You are kind—more so than I deserve. But you do appreciate that I need to stand on my own feet, now I'm widowed, and if I can't do it here, then I must go back to England before too long?'

'That, daughter, you made painfully clear when you left us so abruptly before,' he reminded her without rancour.

She flushed. 'I'm sorry. I *was* sorry——'

He shook his head. 'Not at the time. You were too full of the outraged pride which cannot graciously accept. However, your willing return to us has put that behind us now, and we must do our best to keep you. Let me think——'

Covering his eyes with his hand, he was silent for so long that at last Rowan ventured, 'Perhaps I could work for Cortese Estates?'

The Conte came-to. 'Dario would not agree to that at all,' he said. 'No, I have a better idea. It is this—Before I had my first heart attack, I had been working on a history of the Cortese family and the firm, which I had to abandon while I was ill, but which I could take up again with secretarial help and the necessary leg-work of research being done for me. Yes, I could use a secretary. So why should you not work for me, daughter?' As Rowan looked her surprise, 'For the same figure of salary as you could command anywhere else in the city,' he added quickly.

Rowan said, 'If you think I could, I would

willingly help you with that for nothing,'

'In the intervals of holding down a paid job which would satisfy your ego? What time would you have to spare for fun? For partnering Dario? For being a companion to Lucia?' he countered, smiling. 'No, this we must put on a business footing, office hours and all, if you insist. Even a firm contract, signed by us both, to be broken by either on pain of—on pain of what dire punishment would you suggest?'

They laughed together, Rowan knowing she was committed, but on her own terms, terms which for the first time hadn't been dictated by Dario. She felt almost happy.

Andrea was understandably curious about both Rowan's abrupt departure and return to Rome. As soon as she heard Rowan had come back she collected her and took her to lunch at the Bellini villa while Biron was away.

'No one ever tells me anything,' she complained. 'You were there one minute and the next day you were gone. "Family commitments in England", Zia Lucia told me when I asked, and didn't then seem to expect you back. But now you are here for an indefinite stay and are going to write Conte Arturo's History for him, according to Zia. So what does go now? What is the truth?'

'More or less that,' said Rowan. 'Except that the Conte is writing the history, and I'm looking up old documents for him and typing his drafts

and sorting through sheaves of manuscript he had
worked on already.'

'But do you know enough about the Cortese
family to be able to help him? I mean—old
papers in Italian, can you cope with those?'

'I'm having to learn to,' Rowan admitted, 'the
Conte is a very exacting boss who expects
results.'

Andrea appeared to digest this for a moment or
two. Then, 'Boss?' she echoed. 'You are saying it
is a real job? Not just a way of passing your time?
Whose idea was it?'

'That I should do some work while I'm
here?—mine. That I should work with him on his
book—the Conte's.'

Andrea gave a delicate sniff. 'Sounds like a
manufactured job to me. As if, when he was
afraid you would leave again if he didn't agree to
your working, he hit on this idea of roping you in
on a job he can make as elastic as he pleases; to
last just as long as he needs it to—don't you see?'

'See what?'

'Oh, my dear, it jumps to the eye!' Andrea
scorned. 'At least, it does to mine and must, I
suspect, to Zia Lucia's. Why, that with your
having had no children by Leone, Dario is his
only hope of there being a male Cortese to carry
on the line after Dario. And so—well, work it out
for yourself—the sooner Dario marries any
remotely suitable woman, the better. And since
it's common knowledge that your childlessness

wasn't your fault, who more suitable than
Leone's worthy widow as a marriage partner of
convenience for Dario? Tell me, do you really
mean to say that some notion of what the old man
is up to hasn't occurred to you too?'

Rowan wondered what the effect would be if
she told Andrea, 'It didn't have to occur to me; it
was put to me, forcibly and distastefully, by
Dario himself.' Aloud she said, 'If I'd ever been
tempted to wonder about it, I think I'd have
expected the Conte to be frank with me, and even
more to expect he couldn't harbour any such
plans without getting Dario's consent to them
first. So I'd have dismissed the suspicion as
nonsense. Which plainly it is.'

Andrea sulked, 'How can you be sure Dario
isn't in it too? After all, he is in love with me and
always has been, and as I'm not available, he is
probably none too choosy. Anything female and
reasonably presentable would do. She needn't
even have money, for he has plenty. So why not
you? They may think they have only to keep you
handily on ice until you have forgotten Leone
enough to consider the charms of Dario.' Andrea
paused, then added an arch, 'Or perhaps you
have already considered them—who knows?'

Rowan snubbed that with a dismissing, 'Who
indeed?' and changed the subject to ask after the
progress of Andrea's clandestine affair with her
artist friend, only to hear that it had petered out.

'I'm lying fallow at the moment,' Andrea

claimed. 'Biron thinks I am safe with my pet monkey, Martius Guardia, and so I am—too safe. I do hanker for a bit of intrigue that I have to manage in secret, and when I haven't any on hand, I'm dangerous.'

'Dangerous to whom?' Rowan queried.

'To my girl friends' men, if they don't hold on to them tightly. A dangling man is too easy to catch, which is why you are lucky if there really is nothing romantic going on between you and Dario. For I warn you, I could get him back at the snap of a finger any time I chose——' Andrea broke off, 'But you think I'm wanton, don't you? I know it. Confess!'

Rowan weighed the propriety of insulting her hostess against telling the truth, and came down on the side of the truth. 'Yes,' she said bluntly, and did not care for the sound of Andrea's bitter laugh.

'Of course I asked for that,' Andrea mocked. 'I should have known you belong to the virtuous sisterhood that's never been tempted nor wants to tempt. But if you do ever find yourself falling for Dario, don't hope to make a love match, will you? On his side, it will be purely business!'

Which was rudeness for rudeness, thought Rowan, and with that exchange of candour and sarcasm she and Andrea had declared war.

She had wondered how Dario would view her work for the Conte. But presumably the Cortese prejudice stopped short of its women being seen to 'go out to work', for he seemed to approve it. As he should, in Rowan's opinion, on his father's account if not on hers. For, once launched on the project, the Conte pursued it with all the enthusiasm of a much younger man no longer living on borrowed time. Gradually, as he and Rowan worked regular morning hours on it and sometimes in the early evening, the clutter of manuscript took shape, was annotated and indexed and the Cortese family lore checked for accuracy of dates and details of happenings— marriages, births, deaths and power clashes—of long-gone years. All through the story ran the ugly thread of the curse borne by the senior son of each generation, and Rowan sometimes wondered wistfully how she herself would appear when the history came to the present day. Briefly? Only in a family tree as the childless wife of Leone Cortese, an elder son? After that, nothing about her. In the continuing Cortese legend she would have no place, no story.

The autumn days stretched out, and immediately ahead was the opening night of *Aida* at the Opera House. 'Six or seven of our friends would make a nice party for it,' the Conte ruled happily. 'Say, Andrea and Biron and two or three other couples. Dario will partner you; we shall dine them here beforehand, and you, Rowan, will allow me to buy you your gown for the occasion.'

She thanked him warmly. It would have been churlish to refuse. 'What is more, I shall go with you to choose it,' he pronounced. And he did, escorting her to two or three of Rome's exclusive dress houses before he was satisfied with any. She had pleased him by telling him she must rely on his taste for what would be right for the occasion, and she willingly left him to cajole fitters and saleswomen into achieving a creation which she found enchanting.

The dress was of shell-pink Italian silk, shading to the delicate cream of mother-of-pearl at the hem. The design motif was of shell pleating—the fluted contour of a shell marking the curve of each breast, and larger shells jutting pannierwise at each hip. From its deep corsage to the soft billowing of its skirts, its simplicity was its all, and when she went to join Dario and the others in the *salotto* before dinner on the night, she drew a murmur of admiration such as she had never attracted before. Its effect upon her spirits was as headily intoxicating as wine. For the hours of this one evening she meant to be happy, warning herself that the glittering spectacle of which she would be a part tonight was a one-off experience she would not share again. For the opening of the next winter season at the Opera Dario and Andrea and Biron and the others would be there. But the myth of her belonging in the Cortese circle would be long behind her by then.

At each interval there was a concerted movement of the audience to see and be seen in the foyers and crush bars. People circulated and chatted, and at one point Rowan found herself isolated in a corner with Biron, who kept her prisoner there while he talked.

He had drunk enough to make him voluble, and his theme was grievance against Andrea.

He had a tramp for a wife—did Rowan realise that? There was not a man in their set who was safe from her designs on him. And she didn't confine herself to her own class; she would have an affair with any handsome young *ragazzo* in sight. He suspected her of having one now, though he had no proof. But perhaps Rowan was in her confidence about that?

As Andrea had said her affair with the magazine artist was over and she didn't now rope her in as a stooge, Rowan was able to assure him she was not, and hoped to escape him when the bell sounded to warn the audience back into the auditorium for the next act.

But with his chair barring her way, Biron refused to stir. 'Let them all huddle in like sheep,' he dismissed the rout. 'We can stroll in before the curtain goes up.'

He needed to talk to someone, he complained. He had thought Rowan would help him. She and Andrea were friends, weren't they, and he knew how women *talked*—yap, yap, yap. After that he turned maudlin, recounting some conquests of his own, admitting he was no plaster saint, but——

By the time Rowan was able to stem the tide of his muddled confidences and to shepherd him back to the auditorium they had to run the gauntlet of the ushers' disapproval and to creep to their seats like criminals. Dario, sitting next to her, stirred and frowned without comment, and along the line of seats beyond him she saw Andrea accord Biron an equally cool welcome which, she had to admit, they both deserved.

At the Villa, after the performance, their party gathered for discussion of its brilliance, the merits of the singers and about who had been in the audience and who had not. Andrea pointedly ignored Biron and annexed Dario, claiming he hadn't thrown her the *crust* of a word all the evening. After a time the Conte and Lucia went to bed; other people took their leave and Andrea accepted for Biron and herself Dario's discreet offer of his man to drive them home, as Biron was in no shape for it.

Alone with Rowan, Dario said, 'A pity you seem fated to miss hearing the whole of *Aida*. It's to be hoped you found Bellini compensating company this time?'

'He kept me. He said he needed to talk, and I had to let him.' She had hoped for some word of praise for her ensemble and the poise she knew she had achieved with it. If Dario had been jealous of Biron he couldn't have sounded more piqued. But of course he was only annoyed for Andrea's sake—a thought which put acid into Rowan's tone as she added, 'He wasn't seducing me, if that's what you think.'

'Nevertheless, you were my partner for the evening and Biron had deserted Andrea to go hole-and-cornering with you.'

'Sauce for the goose!' Rowan flashed in English, not caring whether he understood the saying or not. 'Biron's wife can flirt with *you* in front of everyone, but I mustn't spend a quarter of an hour with *him*!'

Dario ignored the gibe at Andrea. He said obliquely, 'A piece of advice? You were a success tonight—grooming, manner, toilette —the lot. Don't let it go to your head. As I've discovered for myself, you have a lot of untapped sensuous potential, but in the matter of experienced allure you are not in Andrea's class. Her husband adores her and she knows it, and if you had any idea of making a dent in his obsession with her, forget it, for you can't win.'

Rowan gasped. 'I believe you *do* think I solicited the tiresome man!' she accused indignantly. 'When I have to go to work on attracting Biron Bellini, that'll be the day! Meanwhile, thank you for the grudging compliments. Cinderella has had her night at the ball, and won't be making any abortive attempts to endanger any of your friends' marriages in future!'

Not looking at him, she waited for Dario's comment on a defiance his arrogance deserved but probably hadn't expected. When it came, it was in an amused, tolerant-sounding drawl. 'But with the night of the ball still young, who could blame two of the uncommitted guests for taking their pleasure of each other—no strings of guilt attached?' he said.

At that she could *not* meet his glance, lest her naked need to believe him to be serious showed in her eyes. He was her enemy; she was his, and yet she wanted him ... craved a warmth they could never share. Against all reason and hope she had fallen in love with him, and only knew it now in this moment of an invitation as cynical as it was insulting.

'If your suggestion is what I think it is, the answer is No,' she told him, proud that at least she wasn't weak enough to yield to it.

She sensed he had shrugged indifferently before following her to the door to open it for her. 'Just an idea,' he said. 'Given a grain of the party spirit, the experience might have had untold possibilities, I'd have thought?'

They were close enough for him to lay a hand on her hip, just above the silk shell pannier. His fingers began to stray towards her breast; must have felt the quiver beneath them. He went on, 'When you take umbrage, I don't know whether you see yourself as misused tragedy queen or a trapped rabbit, but you manage to tremble convincingly. Gratifyingly too—my ego is almost tempted to believe you are afraid of me!'

Rowan drew away from him. 'And you'd like to believe that?'

'With some women it could lend quite a zest to a close encounter,' he said.

Alone in her room, shattered by the contradiction of the resentment to which he roused her and the magnetic appeal which conflict with him had for her, she tried to make sense of an emotion she had never thought she could feel in relation to him.

One hated; one was indifferent; or one loved. She doubted whether any woman could be merely tolerant of a man as forceful as Dario Cortese. Which left hate and love, between which there must be a sharp line of division—surely? Or were all her contentions, all her acrimony, the expression, not of hate, but of an unsatisfied hunger to be valued where she was not? It was a need which turned her to vixenish snarling where in reality she only ached to love and be loved. It was love merging with hate, smudging the line between them. Her body was more vulnerable than her spirit, which explained its yieldings to his attempted ravishment of 'womanflesh' for which he had no value at all.

This evening, just now, if she had sensed any real desire for her in his invitation to make love, in her earlier euphoric mood she might have gone straight into his arms ... But she would have gained nothing from it. Where she was concerned, Dario had nothing to give.

It was Lucia, listening to her radio a few days later, who first heard the news. Rowan waked to

her agitated knocking on Dario's door before he
must have opened to her and drawn her inside.
Through the Villa's thick walls there was no
more to be heard.

It was early, but Rowan got up and, as she
usually did, had gone out on to her balcony to
look at the morning, when Dario came out of his
own french window and across to her.

'I want to leave Zia Lucia with you,' he said.
'She is very upset. Ring for her coffee to be
brought to your room, will you? I have to go to
Andrea; Biron Bellini has been killed outright in
a motor crash on the Turin road. Zia has just
heard it on the news. She wants to go with me to
Andrea, but it's better that I go alone, especially
if I have to break it to Andrea. The news item
didn't say just when it happened, so she will
either be hideously alone or surrounded by
cohorts of reporters.'

He made no reply to Rowan's shocked, 'How
awful!' as she followed him to his room where
Lucia sat on his bed, dragging a handkerchief to a
rag between her trembling hands. When Dario
kissed her and promised, 'I'll be in touch,' she let
him go, and presently went with Rowan to
Rowan's room.

At first she could only reiterate the bald
statement she had heard on the radio, but
stimulated by coffee and gently encouraged by
Rowan, she talked out her suffering for Andrea,
confiding that she had always loved Andrea as a

daughter. A lovely, vivacious girl, childless and neglected wife and now too young a widow, Andrea had been crossed cruelly by fate. Nothing of today's tragedy would have touched her if only she had married Dario. Instead of facing bleak widowhood, she would have been a happy wife and mother. Whereas now——

But as Lucia paused there in contemplation of Andrea's sad future, Rowan noticed a slight lightening of her expression, as of a dawning hope. And though Lucia did not voice it, Rowan thought with a stab of shock that she could guess what it had been.

Andrea, widowed now, would be free to marry again. And Dario, still uncommitted, was free too.

Rowan caught Lucia's eye. Lucia looked quickly away, proving to Rowan that they had had the same thought, thrusting it behind them for the moment, but knowing it would not go away.

They waited for the second news of the morning, without gaining much more detail of the accident. Andrea had been an only child, and her mother was dead after separating from her father who had gone abroad, Lucia told Rowan. 'The child will have no one to turn to. Alone in that great mansion—we must do all we can to help her.'

They dressed and went together to discuss the news with the Conte, who had heard it on his own radio. There seemed an inordinately long time since Dario had left without, as he had promised, telephoning back. They rang the Bellini villa several times, to find the number always engaged. 'The newspapers settling like locusts on the poor girl,' Lucia worried. 'But why does not Dario contact us, as he said he would?'

There was no sign from Dario until late morning, when he returned to be accused by Lucia of failing to bring Andrea with him for comfort and protection.

Dario said shortly, 'Her doctor is with her. She is being sedated and she isn't to be moved until she comes round.' And then, 'She learned of Biron's death less than an hour ago—when she came home, none too sober, after being at a party all night.'

Lucia gasped and protested emptily, 'It can't have been her fault. She must have been detained!' But Dario ignored her to tell his father, 'Biron was off on a business trip; his car ran out of road and overturned on a bend. Andrea left last night for a party with some friends of hers—I don't know them. It seems the thing turned into a poolside orgy. The papers had got the story, and when Andrea was brought home she had to face the reporters of every gutter journal in Rome. There will be scandal, of course. It can't be helped.'

'Though only a nine days' wonder, it is to be hoped,' said the Conte gravely.

Lucia said, 'She will have all our support

behind her. She will be grateful to be able to lean
on you, Dario, and she could hope for no one
better.'

Rowan, watching Dario's drawn unreadable
expression, his lips taut, his eyes banked fires,
wondered what was passing unspoken in his
mind.

Was he pitying Andrea? Judging her? Preparing
to shield her? Recognising her feet of clay as
never before? Envisaging a future with her which
would now be possible? *Loving her still?*

If he were, Rowan knew she had no right to
care. But she did, with a passionate wanting and
jealousy which went to her very core.

CHAPTER SEVEN

DURING the early weeks of her bereavement Andrea wore her widowhood with a frail ethereal dignity, appealing to a pity which soon forgot to censure her. She had a stereotyped plea of 'How could I have *known* Biron would be killed on the night I let myself be coaxed into a bit of a rave party? How was I to blame? It was just cruel, cruel fate,' which dared anyone to suppose she could have anything on her conscience, and soon she was being fêted sympathetically in her rôle of emerging-from-tragedy figure. In private she battened on any help available to her. She could not understand this legal detail; she ought not to be bothered with that. She had *enough* to bear, hadn't she? Was she never to be allowed to *forget*?

Rowan could not have said when she first realised Lucia was working on the thought they had both had on the day Biron Bellini had died. But certainly she was not surprised when Lucia broached the idea aloud.

The Conte, Lucia admitted, had never much cared for Andrea. But even he must see, fate having opened the way, that he couldn't stand in the way of Dario's marriage to Andrea after a decent interval of mourning for her. And seeing his dearest wish was for grandchildren, surely he couldn't want to discourage the marriage, could he? she appealed to Rowan.

'Could it affect Dario's decision to marry Andrea, if he did?' Rowan questioned hollowly.

'No, but it could make for disharmony,' Lucia allowed, adding a more hopeful, 'But as you say, if Dario means to marry Andrea, he will, and Arturo will have to come round. After all, Dario has never looked at another woman but Andrea— That is——' Lucia checked, flushing,—'any in the way of marriage, I mean.' She checked again at another hurdle in her argument. 'Except his offer to you, which——'

'Which of course doesn't count,' Rowan supplied.

'It was an honourable offer which you chose to refuse,' Lucia said stiffly.

'Honourable—a loveless marriage into which I was to be bribed? Could either Dario or the Conte expect me to accept it?' Rowan demanded.

'Nevertheless, Dario would have stood by his word to you, if you had accepted him,' Lucia maintained.

'Then isn't it fortunate for him that I did refuse?'

'Yes indeed—fortunate for both him and Andrea,' Lucia agreed, sounding mollified, but showing by her next question that the bitterness behind Rowan's outburst hadn't escaped her. 'You do not *begrudge* Andrea to Dario? You have

The doctor was disarmingly frank.

'I have not had a professional relationship with Andrea for a long time. Socially, yes, and'—he paused—'more intimately on my side than I ever let her know while her husband was alive. In short, I loved her for years, and now I might have hopes of her marrying me if—well, you have seen them together?—if I hadn't to fear that she will accept Dario if he asks her. As he surely will, now she is free.'

'What makes you think so?' asked Rowan.

A shrug. 'History. Their affair goes a long way back.'

Rowan fastened on a word. 'Goes?' she questioned. 'Do you think that while Andrea was married to Biron Bellini——?'

Another shrug. 'Who knows? I hope not.'

'Well, if you know Dario well enough, I suppose you could ask him if he means to marry Andrea?' Rowan suggested.

Martius Guardia shook his head. 'No. For the same reason, I'm afraid, that I shouldn't approach a man-eating tiger, not sure whether or not he had lunched. Namely, my dear Signora Cortese, that I am coward enough not to want to know the answer!'

'Nor do I. *Nor do I!*' was Rowan's silent echo to that. Doubt was bad enough, certainty would be worse. There was even a kind of consolation to realising that Andrea herself hadn't yet been told the answer.

When they met—more often now, at Lucia's urgings to Andrea to think of the Villa as her second home—Andrea did not return to her argument that the Corteses could be thinking of Rowan as a bride of convenience for Dario. Rowan hoped it was because she had to keep her fingers crossed against the possibility, but thought it more likely that Andrea now saw her as a non-person of no danger to herself, now that Dario would be choosing his own bride after serving his time in wait for her . . .

And yet, though Andrea must know she had all Lucia's backing, Rowan guessed she sensed the Conte's resistance. Rowan might no longer be the enemy, but he was formidable enough to worry her.

'Dario spoils Zio Arturo, defers to him about everything, from business to his personal affairs,' she grumbled. 'Zio Arturo has never liked me, and Dario has always let him keep us apart. I've often thought I'd never have been mad enough to throw over Dario if I hadn't been afraid I'd be marrying the family as well.'

'Though would that have stopped you if you had loved Dario enough?' queried Rowan dryly.

At that Andrea flared, 'And how do you know how much I loved Dario? You weren't here. I tell you, I was crazy about him, as he was about me, and he didn't stop when I married Biron. Why, even then it would have taken very little for him to suggest an affair with him. I had to be very strict with him to show him it wasn't on,' she finished smugly.

'Which didn't stop you deceiving Biron with other men than Dario.' Rowan hadn't been able to resist the comment.

'Oh, *those*! Pff! Just little ploys to stop me from boredom—to keep my hand in at attracting men, as it were. But an affair with Dario would have been quite different—too serious, too demanding altogether. I was a married woman with a jealous husband and an even more jealous lover, and between them they would have torn me apart, no less. No——' Andrea affected a shudder—'even with Dario baying for me, I couldn't risk going *so* far after I was married.'

Though never missing a trick at claiming him whenever you had the chance, thought Rowan. Aloud she asked, 'And now?'—wanting to know.

'Now?' Andrea echoed, sounding innocence itself.

Rowan hadn't wanted to elaborate her question, but—'Well, now that you are no longer a married woman, do you still feel as passionately about Dario as you did?' she said.

Andrea's glance was shrewd. 'I *think* you would rather know whether Dario is still as passionate about me, wouldn't you? Since I was frank with you about my little deceptions of Biron, you've never liked me any more than Conte Arturo does, and probably nothing would please you more than if Dario had cooled towards me. In fact,' Andrea warmed to her theme, 'I wouldn't say you would be above passing on my silly confidences to you in order to influence the Conte even more against me. But just try it, that is all. Just try it, and then watch your spite blow away on the wind. For don't forget—Dario can marry me now, and when he asks me and I accept him there will not be a thing either you or his father can do about it!'

'Then what have you to worry about?' asked Rowan.

Christmas in Rome was a magical experience. On the midnight every carillon, every church bell in the city rang out in great rolling waves of sound, and on the morning itself there was a seasonal diamond frosting on roofs and streets and lawns. For a month before and after it the squares and parks were festooned with lights and the streets turned into open fairs, selling everything from Christmas figurines and cribs to hardware, and from sticky nougat bars to cameras and videos. Christmas lengthened out from the beginning of December to a second highlight event—the children's Fair on the eve of Twelfth Night on the Piazza Navona.

New Year's Eve, with its own bizarre ceremony of everything dispensable, from broken light bulbs to redundant furniture and bicycle tyres, being thrown out of windows, was something yet again. But Epiphany Eve on Navona belonged to the children of Rome.

'There are puppet shows and gipsy pipers who come all the way from the south to be there,' the Conte told Rowan. 'And St Nicholas and Befana, the good witch, and——'

'And noise,' Dario put in.

'But of course noise,' his father agreed. 'Whistles and horns and squeakers and yells. Wherever there are children there is noise. At Cortese Estates we hold a huge party for all the children of our workers and office staff. Dario acts as the master of ceremonies, and after a feast in the boardroom they are given money to spend and loaded into volunteer cars and taxis and taken over to Navona to spend it at the booths. We give them their head for an hour or two, and then round them up and bring them back to the office for their parents to collect them and take them home.'

'In all those crowds, do you manage to find them all?' Rowan asked.

'Give or take a child or two lost without trace, yes.' The Conte paused to laugh. 'No, actually to date, when we have counted them in and counted them out, the numbers have tallied and so have the parents. But it is a great responsibility. You must act as Dario's aide this year, *cara*. He needs one, and you will enjoy it.'

The season was the occasion for a diaryful of visits to and from the family's relatives and friends, all of whom Rowan had not yet met, she was introduced fondly by the Conte, and who accepted her without question as 'one of us'. She had rather dreaded the exchange of elaborate presents within their circle, but was relieved to find this was not so. The Italian gift trade hadn't the enormous volume it had in England; presents were token, rather than extravagant; there was nothing showy about the small cameo which the Conte gave her; she chose a Milanese shawl for Lucia, who gave her an embroidered purse. From Dario she received flowers and perfume, and she gave him an etching of the Arch of Septimus Severus in the Forum which he had admired in a print shop window.

But the Conte made something special of his gift to Dario. It was a ring, a heavy gold band with a ruby set deep in the old-fashioned way, which he wore on his signet finger and now told Dario to wear on his.

'In our family we don't give engagement rings from the man to the woman only. We exchange them,' he explained to Rowan. 'This was Dario's grandfather's ring from my mother and would have gone to Leone if he had lived. Her ring to my father was buried with her, and though I could give this one to you, child, it is a man's ring and too big for you, so Dario must have it instead.'

'Of course,' she agreed quickly. 'It's an heirloom, isn't it?'

'In a way, isn't it?' the Conte appealed to Dario. 'When the woman you choose gives you one, you can keep this to pass on to your son whenever you judge it will fit him.'

Dario fingered the ring, turning it this way and that. 'Or when I judge it isn't in danger of being mistaken for the kind of gewgaw from a chain-store which may be in fashion with the young Roman male by then,' he said.

'Of the Cortese child or children I hope you will have, I find that over-cynical,' the Conte reproved him gravely.

Dario shrugged. 'Cynical or realist?' he queried. 'Any son of mine must have a mother first, and who knows which of us he is going to take after?'

He was looking straight at Rowan as he spoke. Daring her to remember 'womanflesh', she thought. Taunting her that he needn't settle for any such coldly passionless mating now.

'Though isn't it something that a man ought to *want* to know?' The Conte murmured quietly and unanswerably.

On Epiphany Eve Dario and Rowan were leaving for the Estates offices when Lucia and Andrea arrived back from a shopping trip. The four met in the hall of the Villa. 'Where are you going?' Andrea asked Dario, ignoring Rowan.

'To do our stuff at the *bambinos*' party. The usual thing, first the bunfight, then the marketing on Navona,' he said.

'You are taking Rowan? But *you* don't have to stay? I want you to take me to the Scarlattis' party tonight. You could call for me at eight,' Andrea urged.

Dario shook his head. 'Sorry. I'd be lucky to be free by eight.'

'But you knew Mirna Scarlatti was giving a party?'

'Yes, but I told her I couldn't be there.'

Andrea's mouth took an ugly line. 'And I told her you could—that you would be taking me.'

'You could have given me the option of saying No to you as well as to Mirna.'

'On Epiphany Eve I never supposed you would have anything—a business date, for instance— that you couldn't put off or get away from by eight at night. No, Dario, you *must* come. I am going and you can't let me down. I can't possibly face Mirna after promising her I would bring a man—you.'

'I can *not* manage eight,' said Dario firmly. 'You must drive yourself or take a taxi. When everything is cleared at the office I must bring Rowan home, and after that I could go straight to the Scarlattis' at, perhaps, about nine.'

Lucia suggested mildly, 'You could get there earlier if you sent Rowan back by taxi, couldn't you?'

'So I could,' Dario agreed, but not, Rowan noticed with a quirk of satisfaction, as if he meant to entertain the idea at all. For to hear Andrea put to rout on even so trivial an issue as this was, just now, music to Rowan's ears.

The party was all that had been forecast about it—deafening chatter, the floor preferred to chairs for play and sitting around, quarrels, makings-up, baffling shynesses, noisy boastings, infectious laughter, and above all the clatter of plates and drinking mugs and the sporadic pistol shots of bursting balloons.

After the tea, by some miracle of organisation the guests were transported to a man to the Piazza Navona where, with donated *lire* clutched in small hot hands, they were allowed to scatter among the booths, with the promised lure of a Punch and Judy show at a central point at a given time to bring them all together again.

Apparently this worked, for the returning cars were as full as on the outward journey, and the waiting parents and guardians at the office seemed satisfied with the count of the offspring they collected to take home.

At last, in late evening, chaos had gone again—'For another year,' said Dario, and then, his eyes narrowed to peer across the big room, '*Santo cielo*, what is that in the corner there? Not, please heaven, a child that someone has forgotten?'

But it was. Or rather, it was to seem, a child whom no dutiful mother on collection duty had ever owned. For this youngster, a curly redhead of about three, when winkled out of his corner squat, proved to be as stray as a wandering kitten, admitting under pressure that his name was Paolo (without any handle), but either could not or would not explain how he came to have been at the party.

'He is a gate-crasher,' pronounced Dario. 'That's all we need!' He called together the office night cleaners who were beginning on the clearing up. Had either they or the many tea-helpers seen Paolo with anyone, grown-up or other children, at the party? But no one had particularly noticed *one* child among many, and the volunteer car drivers who might have remembered Paolo had dispersed by then.

'We can't leave him here. We must take him home with us,' said Dario.

'But someone will surely remember him and come for him here?' Rowan questioned.

'And how long do we wait on the chance of that? All night?'

'Of course—you have to keep your date with Andrea,' Rowan said quickly.

'It's my guess he is on a lone trip and that no one who has lost him will think of looking for him here. So we could wait until dawn and beyond without result. No, I'll leave a message with the night-watchman to ring the Villa if anyone does come for him or telephone, and we'll take him home and put him to bed.'

During the drive Dario suggested street names and districts with which Rowan plied Paolo in the hope of a clue to where he might live. But nothing emerged, and he was carrying nothing with him but a Christmas crib of icing sugar in one jerkin pocket and a koala bear model in the other. 'Bought illicitly on Navona with our money,' Dario commented. 'However, to bed with him until we are able to solve him, don't you agree? In the spare room of your suite, perhaps? Maria can make up a cot for him there.'

The Conte and Lucia were away, staying with relatives for the feast day, but the kitchen rallied with milk and clucks of sympathy, and Maria improvised a bed with cushions and quilts and unearthed from a long-disused toy cupboard a one-legged teddy bear.

'I did not work here then,' she explained. 'But I have heard it belonged to your husband, *signora*, and after he left Rome, *il maestro* would not permit it to be thrown away. He would like the *bambino* to nestle with it tonight.'

For Rowan the musty toy opened a window on a past she had not shared. When she had been a baby in a London suburb Leone and Dario had been toddlers and teenagers in this palace of an Italian home. The twists of fate had brought first Leone and then Dario into her life, and here in her hands was a childhood link which had survived Leone and, decrepit though it was, would outlive her experience of Dario. Things lingered on when relationships did not. Things without feelings, loves or hates, won every time.

Dario had disappeared after handing Rowan and the child into Maria's care, and Rowan supposed he must have hurried off to his date with Andrea without leaving any directions as to what she was to do if there were a call from the watchman or anyone came to claim Paolo. But she was sitting, watching Paolo struggle against sleep, when Dario joined her again.

'I shot off to the Scarlattis' to beg off for the evening. I shan't be going now,' he said.

'Disappointing Andrea after all? If you'd told me how to get in touch with you if there were any news about Paolo, I could have managed,' Rowan said.

'Yes, perhaps. But now you will be able to go to bed, and I will sit up.'

'I'll sit up with you.'

'Two of us nodding and jerking awake on each other's shoulders? You will go to bed. But before that we'll have supper in your room. What would you like the kitchen to get for us?'

'Oh, just soup and——'

'Soup and something cold and a bottle of wine?' He rang and gave an order, and presently they were sitting opposite to each other at a table in the french window. The Borghese Gardens were ablaze with festival light and under the starlit frosty sky people were still dancing on the lawns.

Rowan remarked, 'In England we finish with most of our festivity at New Year. The only tradition connected with Twelfth Night is that we take down our Christmas trees or we risk seeing ghosts.'

'Risk? I'd have thought the sight of a ghost would be an experience on which one could hope to dine out for months. But after this we sober down too. It is strictly back to business tomorrow, with the next gala excuse being Shrove Tuesday, and for Cortese Estates the Italian Property Owners' Convention, mounted on Rome this year, at which we, the Cortese, are the hosts.'

'It's a very big occasion?' Rowan asked.

'Prestige-wise, yes. The major cities, Milan, Turin, Naples, Florence, host it in turn. The last time it was Rome's turn, Father was in full control at Cortese, but he isn't fit enough now and I shall be in charge.'

'When and where is it held, and what does it entail?'

'At the end of January. Largely out at EUR, in one of its white-elephant convention halls, for meetings and exhibitions of contruction materials and so on. We organise tours of the city's property developments and get together socially for golf and race meetings and evening affairs, and the guests are made honorary members of our clubs for the week.'

'All stag goings-on?'

'Goodness, no! We've some of the best women brains in the country in property management. And there'll be wives and girl-friends attached.' Dario paused. 'I'm lacking a Convention hostess myself. What would you say to taking on the role?' He was passing the bowl of green salad as he spoke, and Rowan took it with shaking hands.

'*I?*' she gasped. 'You can't be serious! You can't possibly consider me——'

'If I hadn't considered you, I shouldn't have mentioned it. I only need your agreement.'

'But there must be plenty more people suitable.'

'More people. Not necessarily more suitable people.'

'That's absurd! You must know somebody you could ask.' What was he thinking of? It was just the part in which Andrea would revel and excel.

'No one with the necessary Cortese connections,' she heard him saying. 'The last time Father officiated for the Rome owners Zia Lucia acted for him as hostess. But she is hardly the contemporary of mine that you are, and there is no one else.'

Rowan stared down at the table. This hurt, but it had to be said. 'In the circumstances, you can't *want* me,' she muttered.

Evidently he understood. 'Knowing what I do of you, you mean? Then perhaps we should agree on a distinction between "want" and "need"? I need you for my hostess. The firm needs you. It will make Father happy—Leone's widow, his daughter-in-law—you mustn't deny him the satisfaction of that.'

She played for time. 'If I weren't here, whom would you choose?'

'You are here and available, so what does it matter?'

Weakening, 'What should I have to do?'

'Act as my hostess wherever I have to host. Receive with me at functions. I'll brief you as we go along. The first big affair will be the opening reception and dinner for the delegates; the last will be the closing ceremony when we—Cortese Estates—will be the guests of honour, and we can sit back and relax. You'll need some day suits for luncheons and two or three different ensembles for evening. Order anything you need and have the accounts sent direct to the firm.'

She gave in. 'If you really think——'

'I've already done the thinking. It's decided,' he said. Gesturing at the table, 'Have we finished here? Would you like coffee or a liqueur? No?' He looked at his watch. 'It's not late, but if you'd like to get to bed, I'll say goodnight and adjourn to the gate-crasher's bedside until something happens for him—or doesn't.'

Rowan took the hint that he had had enough of her. 'You will wake me?' she begged.

'I've had the telephone switched to the corridor extension, so if any news comes that way, you will probably hear it.'

'I'll just look in on him.'

Dario went with her to look down at Paolo, sunk deep into his quilts on his face, both arms flung wide outside them, the maimed bear dangling from a sleep-nerveless hand. 'He'll suffocate,' Rowan whispered, stooping to turn him gently and to retrieve the bear.

'*Hé*, that's mine!' Dario claimed it in surprise.

'Maria found it for him and said it was Leone's.'

Dario laid it beside Paolo and Rowan covered him over. As they left him, 'It was Leone's first, and when he had done with it, it came to me,' Dario remarked.

'With or without his other leg by then?' Rowan asked, amused.

'Already without, as I remember. Handed down to me as damaged, secondhand goods, but I loved him all the same.'

A crippled teddy-bear not the only damaged, secondhand inheritance from Leone to his brother—had the comparison occurred to him that she herself was just such another? Rowan wondered as she padded quietly about her room, undressing. *Or had he deliberately drawn the parallel, meaning her to understand it?* But no, it had been unwitting on his part. For he said he had loved the bear 'all the same'—hadn't he?

She woke to the insistence of the telephone bell and, without slippers or robe, ran into the corridor to find Dario already there, listening and answering.

She stood beside him, hugging her arms in front of her and waiting.

'Yes?'

'Who? Yes, I know her.'

'Where? And so——?' A longer listening, and then, 'Yes, I can find it.' He hung up, saw Rowan and frowned. 'For pity's sake, girl, get *into* something! You'll freeze,' he said irritably. But he had called her 'girl'—sounding concerned for her! He propelled her into her room and followed her in, scooping up her robe, jerking her arms into its full sleeves and kicking her slippers towards her.

'What?' she asked breathlessly. 'Has somebody missed him? Is it all right?'

Dario almost snorted. ' "Little boy lost" indeed! A prize opportunist, that one—he'll go far. Briefly—one of the staff, a young married woman in the typists' pool, sent her two children to the party with a neighbour, but collected them herself after it. The neighbour took her own two along and presumably collected *them* later. So far, so good. But hold on to the thread. It gets tangled when, tonight, a third mother, frantic with worry, goes to Signora Marini's apartment in the same block—her *bambino*, her Paolo, lost without trace since the afternoon. Had Bella Marini—our young woman—any idea where he might be?

'Well, Bella Marini hadn't. But her children had. With them in the taxi which had called for them had been a small strange boy named Paolo. He had got in before the taxi started. They had all supposed he belonged to *someone* and didn't see him again once they arrived at the party.

'One supposes he was able to work the trick

again to get taken to and brought back from the
Piazza Navona. So there you have our pirate Paolo,
on to a good thing with money and prizes and a
good tea and three taxi drives under his belt,
though missing out on the fourth. I daresay he
didn't expect to trip up on that,' Dario concluded.

Relieved beyond measure, Rowan laughed. 'He
will get his fourth if you have to take him home.
Who rang you about him—your night-watchman
at the offices?'

'Yes. Bella Marini telephoned there, sensible
girl. If you will wake him and get him up, I'll be
waiting in the car when you bring him down.
And then get back to bed yourself. I shan't
disturb you when I come back.'

Paolo barely woke when Rowan roused him,
grizzled fractiously while she huddled him into
jerkin and leggings, was asleep again when they
were ready to go. So she wrapped him in a cot quilt
and cradled him in her arms to meet Dario coming
in from outside when she reached the front door.

And then something odd happened. Or rather,
nothing happened as she expected. For instead of
coming forward to take Paolo from her, Dario
just stood watching her with a strange deep look
in his eyes. After a moment of silence he said,
'Woman and Child on Epiphany Eve—only
lacking the Three Wise Men.' And then directly
to her, 'I was right when I told you you chose the
wrong man to marry. Motherhood would have
become you.'

CHAPTER EIGHT

ANDREA's pique at Dario's defection on Epiphany Eve was as nothing compared with her fury over his choice of hostess for the Convention. Both Lucia and Rowan were at the receiving end of her ill-concealed chagrin that she herself hadn't been offered the chance of the role.

Lucia attempted to soothe, 'I think Arturo and Dario felt it to be such a Cortese occasion that Rowan should act. I did suggest—Rowan won't mind my saying this—that, you being so well-known and popular in Rome, and Rowan hardly at all, might be a better choice, but——' Whereupon Andrea, evidently sensing the dice against her, claimed quickly, 'But naturally, if I had been asked, I should have had to refuse. After all, I am barely out of mourning yet. It's just that one would have appreciated being asked.'

'Of course, *cara*, and you must know Dario wouldn't have passed you over if Arturo hadn't made it a matter of business policy to keep it in the family.' Lucia turned to Rowan. 'I'm sure Dario gave you to understand he was asking you because of your being Leone's widow, didn't he?' she appealed.

'If my being told it had already been discussed and decided was "asking" me, yes,' Rowan agreed drily.

Andrea's expression lightened. 'You weren't given the chance to refuse? Dario simply told you you had been *picked*?' She paused to laugh. 'But isn't that just like him? He gives the order and expects you to jump. Which you do.' Another small laugh. 'And will have to, in the name of the precious Cortese prestige—or else. My dear, I don't envy you your hostessing of Dario. At the end of the convention week, you'll be a nervous wreck!'

'Then shouldn't you be glad you had the excuse of your mourning to refuse the offer, if you had been asked——?' a loaded question which Andrea airily sidestepped.

She rose to go. 'Well, do feel free to come to Zia Lucia, or I might be able to help too, if there's anything on the hostess scene you find you can't handle and would hate to admit to Dario that you can't. We Romans are so *very* fussy about social protocol and what is "done" and what is not, you could easily put a foot wrong——' She drifted out, to lunch first with Martius Guardia, then to take tea with a Sicilian countess, and mentioning in passing that it was as well Dario would be busy with convention affairs in the next few weeks, for she would have difficulty just finding space in her diary for a date with him.

When she had gone Lucia mourned for her, 'My poor Andrea! She was so disappointed, one could see. But her pride rides it well, and it wasn't very kind of you, Rowan, to imply she was claiming "sour grapes".'

'Well, wasn't she?' Rowan countered. 'She feels she's been slighted, and won't rest until she's made Dario—or both of us—pay.'

Lucia sighed. 'Dear me, how you and Andrea dislike each other! You could hardly be more averse if you were rivals in love, though when you first came to Rome you were the friends I hoped you would be. Something must have happened to turn you. But of course you catch your hostility from Arturo. *I* am the only friend poor Andrea has in this house.'

'And Dario, surely?'

Another sigh. 'One would suppose so,' Lucia allowed. 'But like all men, he can be insensitive to her finer feelings, so it is not to be wondered at that she rounds on him when she is hurt, as obviously he has hurt her by passing her over for his hostess without any explanation as to why. I suppose——' Lucia hesitated, 'it would be possible even now for you to stand down in Andrea's favour—tell Dario and Arturo that you don't feel you are competent to serve, or something?'

'It could be possible, yes.'

'Then you will try? You will help Andrea?' Lucia pressed eagerly.

'Possible to tell them, I meant—though without a hope of their listening or agreeing. As I've said, the thing was all decided before Dario ever approached me, and you must have long enough experience of them both, Zia Lucia, to know that is the Cortese way—act first, consult afterwards, and then ride roughshod ahead?' Rowan urged.

Lucia's face fell. 'So——' she declared, 'if you won't try to do what you could for Andrea, I suppose I must try myself.'

'Or you could wash your hands of all of us, and suggest to Andrea that she could always plead her own case,' Rowan retorted, not caring much whether she sounded as vixenish as she felt.

She thought she had little to fear from Lucia's efforts on Andrea's part. She herself had been given no choice by Dario, and there was little doubt that the Conte would block any suggestion of Andrea's acting as the Convention hostess. As her days passed in busyness, she discounted any help Andrea was likely to get from Lucia, not realising until later how little Andrea needed direct action from Lucia, as long as Lucia possessed information which Andrea was to find she could use . . .

Meanwhile, ignorant of threat, Rowan began to enjoy herself. As Dario had warned, her role was no sinecure. She had to be briefed and directed herself; she was responsible for the despatch to all the special guests and civic figures of invitations which, by long tradition, had to be handwritten and signed by the Conte, Dario and herself; menus for drinks parties and the opening reception banquet had to be checked and overseen, and in between all this and her work on the Conte's book, she shopped for clothes.

Such scruples as she had against going for luxury and the best were dispelled by Dario's assurance that she would be buying and wearing no more than a *de rigueur* uniform for the job she had to do, and by the Conte's chuckle about the labourer being worthy of his hire. So she went to the best shops, indulging the good taste she knew she had, and deliberately not looking beyond the 'after' of the finishing of the Conte's History, and of her present duty to Dario.

Since their temporary guardianship of young Paolo on Epiphany Eve, and the work they were sharing now, their relations had eased somewhat, and when she needed to hug warmth to herself she deliberately conjured in her mind the little tableau in the hall, herself cradling Paolo, Dario's inscrutable look which had seemed to value her for once, and his first hint of pity for her in her childlessness.

The first sign of danger from Andrea—which Rowan did not recognise at the time—came in the form of Andrea's seemingly casual interest in Rowan's life with Leone in England.

How had they met? How long had they been married when Leone had died? Where had they lived? What family of her own had Rowan, if any?—all questions which Rowan thought would have already been answered in the course of Andrea's gossip with Lucia, and none of them with any conceivable importance until they became more probing, more personal, more barbed.

When Rowan had married Leone had she known about the traditional curse upon the Cortese family's elder sons? Had she been hurt that she had never been invited to Rome until she was a widow? Why had Dario gone to fetch her on Zio Arturo's orders? Here, when Rowan parried the impertinence of the question by saying she had no idea, Andrea opined, 'I'd have expected you to have enough pride to refuse. They didn't want you while Leone was alive, so they could whistle for you now.' She paused there to add archly, 'But of course we outsiders don't know all the facts, do we?'—an invitation to impart 'all the facts' which Rowan did not take up.

During those days before the Convention reception date Andrea was continually at the Villa, too frequently for the Conte's liking, but always welcomed by Lucia and as often— probably primed by Lucia—as she could expect to meet Dario at meals or during his few leisured evenings. Then Rowan was aware of being constantly watched, suspected of an intimacy between herself and Dario which *she* knew did not exist, but which Andrea seemed almost to want to detect, so anxious was she to accuse Rowan when they were alone.

Then, on the actual day of the Reception, Andrea finally showed her hand. She was spending the day at the Villa, going to the Reception as Lucia's guest, and had arrived in a furious temper after being disappointed by her dressmaker in the completion of her gown. It would be finished. It would be delivered in time for the evening, the *couturière* had promised. 'But how can I trust the wretched woman? How do I know that her "in time" is the same as what *I* call "in time"?' Andrea raged, and coming upon Rowan in the *salotto*, was ready to pick a quarrel, Rowan could see. Though how serious a quarrel, how shattering to herself, Rowan was yet to learn.

'Where is Dario?' Andrea demanded brusquely.

Engaged on a small repair to Lucia's evening shawl, Rowan shrugged. 'Today—here, there and everywhere. At the moment, I don't know,' she replied.

'Meaning you don't want to know, because you would rather not have to tell *me* where he is,' Andrea snapped. 'If you had just left him outside that door—' pointing dramatically—'and knew he was still there, you would lie that you had heard him move away. For that's typical—you would go to any lengths to keep us apart, temporarily while you can, and permanently if you thought you had a chance——' She paused to add with heavy malice, 'A chance with him yourself, I mean. For that is what you are up to, isn't it? You have no more shred of feeling for Dario than he has for you. But to be a Cortese of the Villa Cortese and Cortese Estates—that is a chance you don't mean shall escape you a second time, after you missed out on the first. You have Zio Arturo in your palm already, and you can't wait until you have Dario there too!'

Only too conscious of Andrea's hostile glare, Rowan forced herself snip off a thread and inspect her darn before she replied. Then she said, 'I told you, when you asked me about him, that I loved Leone and he loved me. So, since you are convinced I care nothing for Dario, why should you think I would settle for less than marriage to live with him?'

'*Why?*' Andrea echoed. 'Why, because you stand to gain so much more with Dario, of course! When you married Leone he had already been cut off by his father. He'd told you that, you've said. So you had nothing to lose with a love match with him. But *Dario* is another matter. He is the Cortese heir. He *is* Cortese Estates—And besides, knowing that he belongs to me, and always has done, because you hate me, you would go to any lengths to take him from me if you could.'

'Though if he belongs to you, how could I hope to?' Rowan countered.

'You aren't above trying!'

'With what chance of success, if——?'

Andrea nodded menacingly. 'Just as well you realise it, *cara*. For if you tried too hard, I could make you very, very sorry, knowing all I do about you and Leone and the wicked trick you played *for years* on Zio Arturo. Played it for money, didn't you? And got away with it, heaven knows how or why, except, I suppose, that the almighty Cortese pride couldn't bear to let out the secret of how it had been befooled into believing that Leone, the disinherited, had broken the curse, when he hadn't. They told no one. Just the three of them, Zio, Dario and Zia Lucia, swore themselves to the secrecy they've kept until now. But such a pity for *you*, isn't it, that Zia, who happens to care for *me*, should consider I ought to know about it, if I'm to join the family by marrying Dario?'

Rowan knew that the chill of dismay which was freezing her spine must have blanched her cheeks as she realised that, however innocently, Lucia had delivered her—and the Conte and Dario—into Andrea's cunning hands. As steadily as she could she said, 'You'll be gratified to hear that all Zia Lucia has told you about Leone and me is true, except for one thing. I knew nothing whatsoever about Leone's deception of his father in this, and I have evidence to prove it.'

'Evidence!' scoffed Andrea. 'If you have, why has Zia never seen it nor heard it? Nor Zio? Nor Dario?'

Why had she not produced Leone's letter, clearing her, to Dario? For a reason Andrea would not understand. Aloud Rowan said, 'When I first came to Rome I had no proof, but they took my word for it.'

'You mean, when Dario made you come, to confess to Zio Arturo.'

Rowan allowed, 'If you like—made me come. But now you have this information about my past, what do you mean to do with it with the object of harming me?'

Andrea tittered unpleasantly. 'Oh, not only you,' she crowed. '*Principally* you, of course, for daring to suppose you could take my property from me by worming yourself in with Zio Arturo and so with Dario, which Zia Lucia fears you may be succeeding in. But I'm afraid *they* won't escape either the scandal I can stir up about you and your wicked hoax of them which, for reasons best known to themselves, they have glossed over, and accepted you—on the surface. But just wait until the worst gossips in Rome—and I have the ear of most of them, the Contessa Saludo, Signora Vivaldi—begin to put the story around, and then see how soon, though discreetly, the Cortese clan will be rid of you, out of sight and out of mind. Out of *their* sight, and out of the minds of the rest of us—they will *hope*.'

At that, for Rowan, it was as if something snapped. No longer on the defensive from Andrea—the jilt, the facile liar, the marriage cheat—she knew she was going to hit back, and it took her only a reckless moment to decide how.

She said, 'You sound very sure of the power of gossip and scandal?'

Andrea nodded. 'I am. I can be, with a story of this size.'

'Even though Conte and Dario and Zia Lucia have known all about me since I first came to Rome, and have made me their welcome guest; pressed me to stay until the Conte was better, and even after I went back to England, asked me to return? *Would* they have done this if I had deceived them about anything at all?'

'Depends on how cleverly you got round them,' Andrea shrugged. 'As I shall tell it, people will be left to conclude that you did manage to deceive them and betrayed their trust. Which will effectually brand you and make them look simpletons, if nothing more. I'll settle for that.'

'You will put about a story which either Dario or the Conte can pin down as a lie as soon as it comes to their ears?'

'It will be their word against mine.'

'And you think you will be believed? Even though—' Rowan paused on a long breath—'I can tell you that Dario at least trusts me enough to have asked me to marry him?'

There! It was out—the thing she had assured Lucia she would never reveal to Andrea, the thing she had never expected to hear herself voice. No lie on the face of it; Dario *had* proposed marriage to her, and in that flash of decision that she must draw even with Andrea, she had known she meant to use the fact to her purpose. She had deliberately led up to it, stating it in so many bald words Andrea could not fail to understand, and the total effect she had planned was there to be read in Andrea's furious, outraged face.

But, as she knew it must be, her reward would be shortlived. She had bought Andrea's angrily raised colour and incoherent gibbering with her eyes open to the immediate effect of that lying claim to Dario. But she had bought it too dearly. Andrea, at the moment beside herself with dismayed, incredulous rage, had only to calm down sufficiently to take a single question to Lucia or to Dario himself, and she would learn the truth. And what future for Rowan then?

Meanwhile Andrea's protest was an hysterical clamour. 'It's not true! Dario can't have—He wouldn't—He is waiting for *me*. He is mine; he always has been. How dare you try to frighten me with your lies, you——'

But there she caught back whatever ugly word was on her lips as the *salotto* door opened and Dario was there. Again it was a tableau of three— Rowan, with Lucia's shawl draped over her arm, Andrea, breast heaving, graceful fingers balled into hard fists, and Dario, looking from each to each before Andrea darted to him to beat with the fists at his chest while she shrilled, 'She is lying! Tell me she is. Let me throw it in her face that I know she is! For do you know what she has just said to try to torment me! That she is engaged to you, that you have asked her to marry you! Oh, I know she hates me, as I hate her and as you must too. So of all the wild, uncalled-for lies—Dario, it isn't true! It can't be! It—isn't?'

But between those two words she had paused to look at him, and the last one of her questions trailed into silence as he took both her fists and held them down at her waist level before releasing them. Rowan held her breath, waiting. Dario came forward to within a hand's reach of her. Why? To find hers under the fall of the shawl and to take it into his, facing Andrea again.

'We've surprised you?' he asked blandly. 'Not to be wondered at, since Rowan claimed to be surprised herself at the time. But yes, it's true I have asked her to be my wife, and I'm sure she is as sorry as I am that you seem to—mind.'

He must have felt the protesting jerk of Rowan's hand, for his clasp tightened like a vice, indicating, she sensed, that she was to have no part in this drama until he gave her permission to act in it, and then only at his dictation on how it was to go. Andrea was shrilling again, 'I don't believe it! Zia Lucia would have told me——'

'Zia Lucia doesn't know yet. We haven't made a public proclamation of the news.'

'Meaning you have only just——? But if you have asked her, why isn't she wearing a ring?'

'Probably because we've been too busy with

Convention affairs to buy her one. But if it would help you to accept that we are engaged, she shall certainly have one. What about this——?'

Releasing Rowan's hand, Dario took his grandfather's ring from his own hand and slid it on to her third finger, where it hung, a heavy, ill-balanced band. Dario commented to Andrea, 'No jewellers' fit, but as a symbol of engagement it will pass,'—which was Dario being as equally cruel to Andrea as to herself, thought Rowan. Mocking them both. Discarding Andrea, or pretending to. Backing up her own false claim to him, or pretending to, for reasons best known to himself. He had both of them in the palm of his hand like captured moths, and she could almost be sorry she had given Andrea over to his taunting, if she hadn't heard Andrea's flung threats as, reluctant in defeat, she passed Dario on her way out of the room.

'Whether or not this is a wretchedly sick joke, or you have taken enough leave of your senses to engage yourself to *her*,' she hissed almost into his face, 'you are going to live to regret it, and *soon*. All of you. Talk of skeletons in cupboards! The Cortese family has a prize sample that I am going to let out, making you the laughing stock of Rome if you aren't publicly ostracised, and if *she* will be allowed to show her face. And isn't it going to take a braver man than you, my friend, to marry her then?'

There was a strange silence when Andrea had

gone. She might have left behind two dumb people. Whatever questions may have been in Dario's mind, he did not utter them, and Rowan's one need was to flee from the shame she had brought upon herself. At last she pulled his ring from her finger, handed it back to him and managed, 'If you meant that as chivalry, I'm afraid it misfired. I'd lost my head and had lied to Andrea, but I could have faced the consequences when she calmed down. There was no need for you to add to the whole wretched business by lying too. *Nor* for letting her go, believing you meant what you said. That was utterly unforgivable—to both of us.'

Dario said, 'Andrea will find she can weather it, and you brought your share on yourself. What could have possessed you to make her free of our "skeleton", as she calls it? For that is what she was talking about, wasn't it—your trick on my father?'

'Not my trick,' Rowan denied hopelessly. 'And she heard about it from Zia Lucia, not from me. I'm sure Zia meant no harm in telling her, but she is over-anxious for you to propose to Andrea now she is out of mourning for Biron, and she couldn't have known how Andrea would use the story to threaten *me*.'

'Why should Andrea want to threaten you?'

'Because I had been mad enough to make that stupid boast, which I should have had to take back, and probably should have done by now, if you hadn't—interfered.'

'With a confirmation and a proxy engagement ring which, to judge by the lady's exit line, have done nothing to divert her from her purpose of telling all she knows.'

Rowan accused, 'You should never have let her go, believing——'

'She was in no mood to be soothed.'

'You could have done it in a couple of words!'

'By throwing you to the lions? No, once she had the story it was already too late, and if I understand her sense of fun, and I *do*, she will try to pillory us with it, smooth her down as I may. So if she does put it about, we may have a bout of "living it down" before us. Can you face that?'

Rowan said quickly, 'For myself, yes. For your father, no. The story *mustn't* be told of him. That after he knew of the trick Leone had worked on him, he condoned it by inviting me here and foisting me on his family and his friends, seeing them pity me as a childless widow, accepting me, being kind to me—no, Dario, if you can't or won't try to silence Andrea, *I* must. And I think I can.'

'I see. You rate your persuasive powers higher than mine? How do you propose to go about it?'

'By confessing that I was lying, of course. And telling her I know you were only playing a cruel joke.'

'And if you don't succeed, do you credit Father with less spirit to ride a family scandal than you have yourself?'

'But don't you see,' she pleaded, 'I *must* grovel to Andrea, because I can't risk the story's hurting him . . . breaking him? And you shouldn't risk it either.'

Dario said coldly, 'Thank you. You can leave my filial duty to me. Very well, try your hand at confession and persuasion. But I ask just one thing—that you let today's sun go down on Andrea's current wrath. Don't tackle her tonight. Go to her tomorrow if you must. But not before.'

'How can I rest in the meantime? Andrea will be at the Reception, and could be planning to spread the gossip there!'

To that Dario ruled crisply, 'You are not meant to rest tonight. You have an evening's strenuous socialising before you, and I'm expecting you to sparkle, no less.'

'I can't *go* to the Reception—after this.'

'Not go?' He turned on her. 'Nonsense. Of course you will go.'

'Andrea is dressing here and driving Zia Lucia in her car. I must see her before that and make my peace with her. She must *not* get a chance to talk!'

Dario said, 'If you try to see her, I wash my hands of you. If you obey me, I'll see that Zia ensures Andrea holds her tongue. In any case, you have little enough time for placating Andrea. You should be dressing yourself now. You and I must be there an hour before the first guests arrive, so I'll expect you to be ready in——' he looked at his watch—'say, an hour from now?'

But a very little short of an hour later Rowan was still sitting on her dressing-stool, nothing but her bath taken and her evening make-up done. The slip and dinner dress of aquamarine watered silk which Maria had laid out for her remained untouched on her bed. They were not going to be worn tonight.

She had left the shawl in Zia Lucia's empty room and had come to her own, seeing no one on the way. At first she had gone about her preparations mechanically, keeping her mind a blank. But now, at only the strapless bra and panties stage of her dressing, her will was at work. She would not, *could* not go to the Reception as hostess to Dario—to stand at his side, to receive, be introduced, to be fêted as a kind of consort to him in the Cortese world of business—when she had handed to Andrea the key to the disgrace Andrea had promised they would all share when she chose to tell her story. Dario might think he could gag her for twenty-four hours, but sooner or later she would tell it. Rowan had no doubt of that, and in face of the threat which her mad boast had caused to hang over them all, Dario expected her to 'sparkle.' *No!*

There was a knock on her door. She waited. 'Who's there?' she called. No reply, but a second knock, peremptory this time, reminding her of another night when her answering had admitted Dario, bent upon violation as a punishment he meant to exact, and she shivered. If he had come to find her now it could only be in impatience and the frustration of waiting for her, but for the result of her decision not to go with him she trembled. She had made it as much for his sake as her own, but she doubted if she could justify it to him. He was not going to understand . . .

She called again, 'Who's there?' and was answered, as she knew she would be, by Dario's entry. He was in formal dress for the evening, cloak careless over one shoulder, evening scarf in his hand. At sight of her unreadiness he sloughed the cloak and dropped the scarf on to her bed and came to stand over her, his angry eyes meeting hers in the mirror they both faced.

'And so—demand my apology for intruding in your room, and you have it,' he said. 'But why aren't you dressed? We ought to have left already. How much longer are you going to need?' And then, as if he read the message of her hands, idle in her lap, 'You aren't trying to get ready! Why not?'

She couldn't continue to look at his reflection. 'Because I don't need to dress for tonight. I'm not going to the Reception,' she said.

She had been prepared for a shocked echo of her words, but not for his near-daemonic laugh and the cruel bite of his fingers into her shoulder as he spun her about on the stool and brought her unsteadily to her feet. Through gritted teeth he muttered, 'You are going, if I have to drag you by the hair, or even if you dare me to take you as you are—in your underwear. So choose—get into those things which have been laid out ready for you, or I'll force you into them myself.'

She shook her head. 'No.'

'*Yes!*'

'No, I can't—You must make an excuse for me—say I'm ill——'

'Coward,' he taunted her. 'I'm not lying for you, just because you're afraid of Andrea.'

'I'm not. It's not that——'

'What, then? Hurry!'

'It's—oh, Dario, try to understand! It's that, even if Zia Lucia can persuade Andrea to keep quiet for the moment——'

'She has done rather better than that. She was so floored by Andrea's betrayal of her confidence that she has told Andrea it would be tactful of her to absent herself from the Reception. So Andrea won't be there.'

'You didn't tell Zia Lucia what—what drove Andrea to it?' Rowan breathed fearfully.

'No. But go on. If you aren't letting me down because of Andrea, what gives you the idea you have the right?'

'Because I *have* the right. It's my duty to shield you and your father and Zia from the consequences of the Leone story when it comes out, as Andrea will see that it does sooner or later, and then people—your friends, your business colleagues—mustn't be able to remember that the woman who was your hostess for the Convention was the one who had cheated and lied to you, *and you had let her hookwink you*—and them. But if I'm not there, and leave Rome, as I mean to as soon as I can, they will forget me and will forgive you the sooner for having ever accepted me, don't you see? Dario, please try?' she begged.

'Try to solve a possible future situation by snarling up a very present and important one tonight?' He shook his head. 'I've listened to you. Now you will listen to me. Rome *needs* this Convention. The whole property industry of the country, which builds and renovates homes for people, needs it. I've worked to make it a success and you have done your share. Tonight and during the coming week we aren't merely playing golf and meeting over the soup and fish. We are exchanging ideas and discussing the future. In other words, *working*, and at this stage I'm not having you back down on your promise to do your part. I am not—I repeat, not—making feeble excuses for your absence tonight or from any other duty you may want to leave undone. Do I make myself clear—or not?'

Rowan murmured wretchedly, 'If you force me, you'll play straight into Andrea's hands, and you're going to regret it.'

'That will be my problem.'

'And your father's, and Zia Lucia's.'

'Possibly. But now, since you've permitted me

to see you in half dress, may I take it you are
going to let me help you with the rest?' His tone
had lightened to raillery.

'No. Please go. I'll——'

But he had moved to the bed, had picked up
the slip and now brought it to her. 'A novel
experience—dressing a woman,' he remarked.
'*Un*dressing them is much more exciting!'

CHAPTER NINE

DARIO had got his way and could afford to let surface pleasantry take over from anger. He had persuaded Lucia to silence Andrea for tonight and was himself punishing her malice until he chose his own time for silencing her for good by convincing her that Rowan's claim to him had been a hoax and his part in it merely mischievous.

He must know he couldn't wait too long, thought Rowan. But that was the way it would go, and that would be the way of a future Rowan would not be there to see—Andrea, forgiven all her petty treacheries and taken back like a repentant child, would have Dario in thrall again to a desire whose flame she had been illicitly fanning for years, jealous of its ever flickering out. On his own showing, Dario was no monk, and she must have been afraid for it many times. But he had married nowhere else; Andrea could be in little doubt he had been serving his time for her.

But tonight he was all debonair courtesy to the woman whose duty to him he had forced, displaying her as proudly as if he really valued her, and Rowan allowed herself to bask in the acclaim he was sharing with her.

They had earned it. The glittering occasion was a tribute to the work they had put in, and Rowan felt that, whatever harm Dario considered she had done to the Cortese family, at least he was allowing her to make up for it in the help he was asking of her now.

The immense white building was filled with light and music and movement and talk and conviviality made easy with wine. Introductions were made, thumbnail personal histories exchanged, common interests discovered and discussed, future dates made and the evening's dinner partners paired. At the top table of three Dario was entertaining the guests of honour, the Conte seated at his right side, Rowan at his left, Behind them hovered the toastmaster, primed and ready for his call.

At the end of the meal there were speeches inviting applause and laughter, some of it polite, some warm and appreciative. When Dario rose to his feet there was a stir of anticipation. A speech from the presiding sponsor of the Convention was evidently expected to be full of meat, and Dario was known to be a good raconteur. He spoke of the year's achievements and the aims and hopes of their industry. He paid generous tribute to everyone who had worked for its success, and was heard with rapt attention. And then, a shade diffidently, he added, 'And talking of things accomplished, I'm bold enough to invite you to be glad for me in a personal triumph of my own. So meet, will you, not merely my Convention hostess who has already charmed you, but the lady, my late brother's widow, whom I have asked to be my wife——' His hand, held out to Rowan, drew her to stand beside him, when his arm went round her waist.

Breathlessly she had glanced at him to see nothing she understood in his face. Tomorrow he would be denying her in order to placate Andrea's fears. Tonight he was making public claim to her. *Why?* Impossible to create a scene by an equally public rejection of his words. She had no choice but to stand there with him and pretend acquiescence and a newly-betrothed happiness she would be expected to feel. She looked past him to the Conte, who was smiling complacently, as if he was sharing none of her own bewilderment, as if Dario hadn't surprised him at all . . .

Dario's lifted hand was quelling the uproar of congratulations and eager questions which surged about him. He was saying, 'You will allow, I've no doubt, that I've probably had a busy day. But I had to find time in it to shop for—this,' as he snapped open a ring-case to reveal a huge solitaire diamond embedded in its velvet. Rowan gasped, and amid the envious 'Ahs' of their nearest women guests, he put it where his grandfather's had briefly rested earlier. He bent to drop a light kiss upon that finger, and then kissed her warmly on the lips in a show of tenderness she would have given anything to believe he meant.

There was stir now as people left their places at the tables to mingle again. Under cover of a small lull in their vicinity she clutched at Dario's sleeve. '*What*——?' she begged of him.

He shook his head. 'Nothing for now. We've an image to maintain. Later. Please wait,' he said. Which told her nothing, but he detached her grasping fingers quite gently, and in the enigmatic words there seemed to be more promise than threat. The astonishing evening had to be finished according to plan. But later? Afterwards? Though it couldn't be an engagement ring, the many-faceted jewel on her finger had to have some well-intentioned meaning behind it, hadn't it? Surely? she hoped. Or, the bleak thought intruded, could it be another attempt to trap her into a marriage of convenience? That would account for the Conte's appearing to know all about it. But what need for Dario to marry anyone other than Andrea, now she was free?

At last it was over. Before the Conte had left early with Lucia, Rowan had purposely avoided him, reluctant to hear any explanations but Dario's. Now they had accepted the last congratulations on the evening's success and had shaken their last guest by the hand. Dario's man had brought up their car and they sat side by side in its shadowed depths, neither speaking, as if, with too much to be said between them, they

could not find the words. Rowan had still said
nothing, asked nothing, when in the hall of the
Villa. Dario said, 'If I may, I am coming up with
you, *amante*,' and linking his fingers into hers,
led her up the stairs.

Amante? Sweetheart?—addressed to her from
him, when they had no image to live up to, no
false parts to play? This wasn't happening—it
couldn't be! But it was. In her room Dario
slipped her cloak from her shoulders and putting
her into the antique curved love-seat which
graced the window embrasure, he stood before
her, making play with her fingers, lingering to
turn the diamond to catch the light.

He was calling her sweetheart again and,
'Thank you for making this easier for me,' he
said. 'Nothing further from your thoughts, I
know, but——'

'This? Easier? What?' she echoed blankly.

'Claiming you, of course. I didn't suppose you
meant a word of your boast to Andrea, claiming
me, but I made capital out of it by backing you up
and keeping you guessing until I could find the
time and the place for asking you to marry me,
hoping you would say Yes, because I'd have
convinced you that this time I was asking you for
love. I've been meaning to for too long and
wouldn't have held out much longer. But then
Father took a hand, suggesting I claim you first
and make love to you afterwards. Claim you so
publicly that you couldn't refuse, without making

both of us look fools. Which was good thinking as far as it went, except that it dealt with the asking, but not with the answer. And it's that answer I'm having to beg of you now. Rowan? Please?'

She shook her head bewilderedly. 'Your father knows you think you're in love with me?'

'Correction—*am* in love with you. Yes, he has known for some time.'

'But when did he——?'

'Ah—well, as our audience was ready to believe, I've had a busy day. After our fracas with Andrea, there was Zia Lucia to brief, and Father to co-opt and a salesman from the State jewellers to bring up to the Villa with samples——'

'But—Andrea?' Rowan questioned. 'You were cruel to her and about her this afternoon. But she is your woman and you'll forgive her. You can't want her *and* want to marry me, unless——'

'Unless on the same terms as you refused before?' he finished for her.

'When you and your father thought you could buy me, yes.'

'And were as wrong as you are being now, beloved.' He stood back, spreading his hands and squaring his shoulders. '*Cielo!* Was Father right when he warned me you might not believe me, and that I should have to *show* you? If so—come then. I'll *make* you believe—know—experience . . . Come!'

She stood up and moved to him, made reckless by a need of him that was stronger than her will.

His arms were inviting her, his lips waiting. To snatch at the Now of his desire and her own she didn't have to believe he loved her, did she? To fuse with him, however briefly, for a few blessed moments of time would be all she asked.

In his embrace she was all yielding pliancy, the curve of her body moulding to the pressure of his. His mouth moved on hers, his hands wandered, explored, caressed; a forefinger traced a line from temple to jaw and throat as if in a blind memorising of shape. Then from the gentle homage of that, he turned arrogant again, frightening her with barely reined passion—and reality returned.

Panting, at anti-climax, she accused him unjustly, 'What did that prove? You assaulted me in much the same way that other night, and certainly not for love!'

He had released her, and when she sank back on to the love-seat he came to sit beside her, crowding her, the hardness of his thigh through the silk of her gown a kind of mastery in itself. He agreed imperturbably, 'To punish you for name-calling, as I remember. "Stud"—you couldn't have kicked me into a much deeper gutter than that, and you meant it. And yet I had the crazy idea that you wanted me. You hated me and you fought me, but your body at least wanted me. Did it?'

Rowan avoided his eyes. 'Achingly,' she said.

'Ah, darling——'

'But *you* hated me. You left me in no doubt of that from the day you met me.'

'When I thought I had every reason to hate what you and Leone had done.'

'Yet with still no reason to forgive me or believe I was as innocent as I said, how can you claim you love me now? It doesn't—fit.'

Dario laughed drily at that. 'My sweet innocent, we aren't living a neat jigsaw puzzle with all the pieces intact and ready to fit. We are living *life*, full of contradictions. I hated what you had done, but loved you for what you were—I think, from that very first day in London. I don't know. I'm not sure about that. But later, when you made a dare of your defiance of me I knew I loved you—for your spirit, your lovely body, even your loyalty to Leone, everything about you. And you—even when you hated me, you couldn't stop your body from answering mine, saying No and Yes to me at the same time and meaning them both—somehow. Nothing of a logical pattern about that. Just two people illogically in love, being—human. You see?'

She nodded slowly. 'I—want to.' But at the swift turn of his shoulders she stopped his reaching for her. 'When I knew the truth, I didn't feel very loyal to Leone,' she went on, 'and I'd have given anything to be able to prove to you that you were wrong about me. But as soon as I began to let myself know I loved you, I'd have given just as much for you to trust me without

any proof. But I have proof now, if you want it—
a mislaid letter from Leone, to be opened——'

He turned fully now to take her into his arms
again. 'And you can keep it, or burn it, or make it
into paper-chains,' he murmured. 'Though I
wouldn't admit it, I took your word long ago.
Even on the night when I kissed you in your
sleep and called you a liar, I qualified it with
Darling—not that you heard—What now?' he
questioned as she jerked free, holding him off.

'The night I collapsed at *Aida*? But you didn't
kiss me! I'd dreamed that, and what you said,'
she declared.

'H'm—funny, isn't it, that we should agree it
happened?' he commented.

'Only in my dream!'

'Then if you only dreamt it, how do I know
what I said?' he demanded unanswerably, as his
mouth silenced her protest in a long, hungry kiss.

It was the first of many to which she responded
as greedily, not now in the desperation of
unreturned love; now instead, in totally shared
physical delight, in given and taken promise and
in the wonderment of possession.

She hadn't now to snatch and regret, nor to
despise the surge of passion which this man
aroused in her. There was going to be a time for
indulging it without guilt, for enjoying it and for
knowing it would have the power to fling them to
the heights of ecstasy again and again.

And so she kissed and was kissed, her senses

teased and stimulated, her willing surrender to the urge of his body made sure of, if not consummated. There was a point in time when Dario's deep gaze held hers and he questioned, 'Now?' and she understood him. But tempted as she was, 'Not yet. Not until——' she said in a kind of lovers' shorthand which spoke more than it said, yet was still understood.

They sat close at last, fingers entwined, their tides at an ebb of content and peace. Dario pointed out, 'You haven't said yet, "I love you, Dario Cortese".'

Her smile was gentle, a caress in itself. 'I love you, Dario Cortese,' she obeyed him, and for good measure, 'Love you, *love you*.'

' "And will marry you as soon as you can arrange." '

'And will marry you——' She broke off in remembered panic. 'Andrea—is she going to *let* us marry in peace from her tongue?'

He nodded reassurance. 'She will hold it. When she comes to her senses she will know she dare not risk wild slander at our expense.'

'She threatened *me* with it.'

'Only threatened—to frighten you out of your claim to me. I was her property, she considered— hands off!'

'And I thought you were. Everyone said so, and that after Biron died, you would marry her.'

Dario said slowly, 'There was a time, a very long time ago, when I loved Andrea and would have married her. But never since then. Never since the day she sent Bellini to me to tell me they were lovers and were going to marry, not having the common courage to tell me herself. That was the death of my love for Andrea, and I sent Bellini back with a message to say that he had been at the funeral.'

'If he ever gave the message to her, she didn't believe it.'

'Such a pity for her best-laid plans, and I have to confess that since Bellini's death, I've rather enjoyed keeping her and everyone guessing until tonight, when our announcement made at least one of our audience happy.'

'Somebody other than me?'

'You? You weren't happy—you were outraged!' he taunted her. 'No—Andrea's pet follower, Martius Guardia. He was there as somebody's guest and he buttonholed me afterwards to tell me he is leaving Rome to set up practice in Milan and that he plans to ask Andrea to marry him. As things have fallen out, I imagine she will accept him, once the novelty of widowhood wears off.'

Rowan shook her head. 'There's nothing novel or exciting about widowhood. It's a kind of setting out across a desert without even a water-bottle or a map.'

'A desert you haven't to fear any more. From now on you have me and a whole caravanserai of Cortese family along with you,' Dario consoled. He paused. 'I wonder—What would you say to our going together to Father to ask his blessing on—all this?'

'Oh—— Now? Tonight? It's very late, he'll be asleep,' she demurred.

'I think he may wake enough to welcome us. Shall we go?'

The tall uncurtained windows of the long corridor showed the expanse of the Gardens, the lawns almost white in the full moonlight, the tree-shadows darkly etched like fretwork. Far beyond, Rome still hummed and glowed, but out there everything slept, as did the great house to which Rowan had come guiltily all those months ago. Like its people, it had appeared as her enemy then, a place of dangerous cross-currents and pitfalls. Yet, like its people, it had come to be loved and yearned for as the unattainable home which, because Dario loved her, it was going to be for her now.

The Conte's room was dark. Inside the door Dario signalled silence with a finger at his lips as he left Rowan to go to bend over his father's bed. Then his hand beckoned her to go to stand beside him, where his arm went round her as he whispered, 'Father? I have brought Rowan to you—with love. You are glad?'

For long moments the old man gave no sign of having heard. He lay as still and unaware as he had lain for so long in his coma. Then his eyelids fluttered and his breathing changed rhythm. His hands stirred and found their way out from under the covers, while his eyes sought focus for their shadowy figures. Next there was a drowsy smile. 'Dario ... and Rowan. That is good,' he said quite clearly. And then on a fading murmur to Rowan, 'Now, daughter, we can both forgive Leone for the wrong he did us. You will have all the love you deserve from Dario, and for me, the old one, it is enough to hope that the line will go on——'

His voice trailed away. He was asleep again, and they left him so. Outside his door Rowan breathed, 'When he calls me daughter, I glow. From him to me it's a lovely word.'

'But I know a still lovelier one for you,' Dario said. 'Wife.'

If *YOU* enjoyed this book,
your daughter may enjoy

Keepsake

Romances from

CROSSWINDS

Keepsake is a series of tender, funny, down-to-
earth romances for younger teens.

The simple boy-meets-girl romances have
lively and believable characters, lots of action
and romantic situations with which teens can
identify.

Available now wherever books are sold.

ADULT-1